When the Sails Go Up and the Waves Come Ashore

Lila B. Mullins

PublishAmerica
Baltimore

© 2002 by Lila B. Mullins.
All rights reserved. No part of this book may be reproduced in any form without written permission from the publishers, except by a reviewer who may quote brief passages in a review to be printed in a newspaper or magazine.

First printing

ISBN: 1-59129-585-8
PUBLISHED BY PUBLISHAMERICA BOOK PUBLISHERS
www.publishamerica.com
Baltimore

Printed in the United States of America

Dedication

To a woman of unwavering faith,
my daughter,
Lynn M. Williams

To: Sharma —
My friend —
for your quiet
moments.

Leila B. Mullins

Acknowledgements

Thanks to the many who have encouraged me and have taken a special interest in my writing.

My sincere gratitude to a loyal friend, Trish Hodgson, who has encouraged me every step of the way. She followed the development of the story weekly, and her enthusiasm kept me going when I was beset with a dry spell. Also, many thanks to her for introducing me to Mary Carrigan.

A double measure of thanks to my typist and public relations agent, Mary Carrigan, who always goes the extra mile. She never came to a bridge she was unable to cross or a wall she was unable to scale. Nothing is impossible with Mary. For her a dead end is only a detour to a better way. She leaves no stone unturned and no path is too difficult. Her assistance has been invaluable; her dedication is a blessing.

List of Major Characters

Lilly Tompkins	Story teller
Larry Mathis	Environmentalist at "Protect the Earth" Foundation
Teresa	Larry's wife
Tony Saunders	Owner of "Saunders Projections"
Jack Longley	Curator of art gallery
Alexander and Josie	Caretakers at Canaan
Cecil	Artist at Sea Haven
Miriam	Cecil's wife
Maudie	Old woman at Sea Haven
Laura and son, Billy	Residents of Sea Haven
Luke and son, Nathanael	Owners of fishing schooner at Sea Haven
Mr. Adkins	Owner of General Store in Sea Haven
Joshua	Sea Haven errand boy and news carrier
Amanda	Nathanael's wife
Iris Gallagher	Girlfriend (later, wife of Billy)
Peter and Naomi	Caretakers at Eden
Ruth and Jason	Daughter and son of Larry and Teresa
Sabrina	Ruth's adopted daughter
Lee	Gardener at Eden

Preface

This is the story of Lilly, a thirty-two-year-old woman who, after the death of her husband of ten years, leaves her home in Charleston, South Carolina, to start a new life in Santa Barbara, California.

Lilly joins the faculty of a small university, never suspecting that an exciting journey is about to begin. Soon she meets Larry, an environmentalist, who persuades her to accompany him to Africa and assist in making a documentary on land erosion. He proves to be a gentle yet forceful man with high moral standards, never wavering.

Later Lilly and Larry travel to Washington State in search of a remote fishing village where they hope to find the artist Cecil. Gradually, the villagers of Sea Haven become an important part of their lives: Mr. Adkins, owner of the General Store; a young boy named Joshua, a slow learner who is the village errand boy and news carrier; Laura and her son Billy; Nathanael, the fisherman; Old Maudie, a very colorful character who makes doughnuts for the children; and of course, Cecil and his wife, Miriam, who become close friends with Lilly and Larry.

As the villagers gather at the Fish and Chips Diner, the conversation often includes the story of the mysterious "Water Baby." After a few years the mystery is solved.

In the meantime, Lilly meets Tony, a businessman who owns "Saunders Projections." He has a beautiful home called "Canaan." Alexander and Josie are caretakers of his property. A relationship develops between Lilly and Tony. He brings her happiness in a way she never thought possible.

Many other people appear on the scene including Teresa, a brave woman battling a life-threatening bacterial infection; Lee, who is Larry's gardener at his home, Eden; and caretakers, Peter and Naomi.

Jason, Ruth, and a charming young girl, Sabrina, affect Lilly in a surprising way.

The story of Lilly spans a twenty-five-year period and is filled with varied events as she travels different roads with many turns and uncertainties. It demonstrates the way circumstances and people influence our lives in a unique manner, teaching us compassion and understanding.

This is also a story of adventure, love, sorrow, pain, joy and mystery. As we watch Lilly mature we see a woman who lives and loves passionately yet remains focused and embraces values that perhaps we would like to emulate.

Chapter 1

There was a subtle hint of approaching autumn in the air that late summer morning when we stopped to absorb the panoramic view. I had never been to Washington State, which was quite a contrast to southern California and different from the southeastern United States, where I grew up. The scenery was breathtaking and for a brief moment I wished I could stay in this place forever. Larry and I had flown in from Los Angeles to Seattle at dawn and were now driving south in search of a remote fishing village.

"I never want to leave here," I said.

"It is beautiful," replied Larry, "almost like a different world. I think we have an exciting adventure ahead of us."

We met eighteen months ago when Larry came to the university where I was a lecturer on family relationships. I'm also a writer, and he hoped I would assist him in preparing a documentary on conservation.

"There's a man in the hall asking to speak with you," said one of my students. "He's working on a project you may be interested in."

"Show him to my office. I'll be there in a few minutes."

He was looking out the window when I came in. He turned as I approached, extending his hand and displaying the most beautiful smile I had ever seen said, "I'm Larry Mathis." I was almost speechless, which is unusual for me, and I stammered, "I'm Lilly Tompkins."

His eyes were light brown to green, his hair brown with some gray. He was tall, muscular and rugged—the most beautiful man I had ever seen. A blush crept across my face as I tried to regain my composure.

"Tell me about your project," I managed to say.

Larry described with great fervor his concern for our planet—soil erosion, destruction of our rain forests, failure to protect our natural resources.

"I'm hoping you will agree to go with me to an area that is being stripped of trees and plant life where animals no longer have a home."

"How could I possibly help in an undertaking of this magnitude?"

"As we walk through the devastation, you can describe what the camera crew is recording on film."

"I don't think I'm capable of participating in this project. My area is family relationships—men and women understanding each other so that they can be happy and well adjusted in this world."

"But if our natural resources are destroyed, there will be no life."

It was very difficult for me to keep my mind on erosion when this man was standing so close, yet the seriousness in his eyes, the passion in his voice, his entire being consumed by his concern, jolted me back to the issue at hand.

He was saying, "I heard your lecture this morning. I've read your articles in *Relationships Magazine*. I know you can transfer your enthusiasm to this project."

"May I have a few days to think it over?"

"Of course, how about dinner Friday evening, if you don't already have plans?"

"Fine. I'll look forward to it."

I handed him my business card and he again flashed the most beautiful smile I had ever seen.

He was gone and I was trembling.

Who is this man? Is he married? No wedding band, but that doesn't always mean anything. Three days until Friday.

Dinner was pleasant, beginning with small talk. Finally, Larry launched into the details of this project. He planned to go into remote areas where trees were being removed for so-called progress. The land was being ravaged of all life-sustaining plants, trees, soil—wildlife threatened—the entire ecological system interrupted.

The trip would last three months. A two-man camera crew would film and a few natives would go as guides. Larry and I would provide the commentary.

I hesitated, but asked anyway, "Do you consider the trip dangerous?"

"Accidents occur in any kind of travel, and the companies cutting down the trees won't look kindly on our research, but otherwise I don't expect any problems."

My adventurous spirit was being awakened and I said, "I would have to take a leave of absence and hope the university would allow me to go."

That smile again, and Larry saying, "I don't think you'll ever be sorry. It's an opportunity of a lifetime. The worst part will probably be lack of sanitary conditions. We will operate from a base camp, a lodge staffed with doctors, nurses, cooks, good clean beds, and all the comforts of home, but we won't be able to come back to the base camp every night. Maybe once a week."

I was overwhelmed with the thought of it all, but also compelled to go. My life had been humdrum long enough.

"Larry, do you have a family?"

"Yes, I have a wife and two children. Teresa is an architect and artist. She designs buildings all over the world. Jason and Ruth are in college. What about you?"

"My husband died twelve years ago, so I decided to move west and start a new life. I've become completely absorbed in my writing and teaching."

"No social life?"

"That's right."

"You know the saying, 'All work and no play makes Jack a dull boy and Jill very lonely.'"

I thought, was I lonely? Maybe so. Perhaps this was the reason this mission seemed so appealing to me.

We had two and a half weeks to prepare for the trip. Every now and then a tinge of apprehension came over me, but disappeared as I looked forward to the unknown.

When we arrived at the base camp on the other side of the world we were greeted by Dr. Evans, Dr. Brown, three nurses, and two uniformed black men, officials of the government who were assigned to the conservation office. Also, several native men were standing at a distance, anxious to see the arrival of strangers.

The headquarters building was nicer than I had anticipated. It resembled a lodge or a long ranch style house. One wing was the infirmary, which at that time housed only two patients. A woman who had given birth prematurely was being treated for anemia. Her baby was small, but doing well. The other patient was a very old man dying of cancer.

My room was large with two windows at the back overlooking a vegetable garden and a few exotic plants and flowers. The bed was very inviting, neat and clean. I probably could have slept several days.

We had orientation for two days and an inspection tour on the third day. With a map indicating the locations of areas destroyed by heavy machinery, we were ready to begin our documentary. Our group consisted of two native guides, Achu and Lomin, who spoke only minimal English, two camera men, Eric and Paul, Larry and myself.

Our Land Rover was fully loaded the day we left base camp. We had camera equipment and supplies including tents, a small stove, and everything needed for living temporarily in the open.

The destruction of the land was more drastic than indicated by photos and I was anxious to get started with the filming so the entire world could be informed of this disaster.

Larry and I had decided to do the audio in conversational style as the cameras rolled, and the damage was easy to describe in explicit language.

Everything was going smoothly and on schedule. We returned to the lodge on the weekends for hot baths, comfortable beds and good food.

Our good fortune was too good to last, I guess. In the middle of the seventh week I had an accident. Walking on rocky terrain I fell after stepping on a loose rock, and another large rock rolled over my ankle and foot. Crunch! I knew my foot and ankle were broken, and I cried out in pain.

Achu and Larry reached me first. They removed the rock from the top of my foot. Achu was screaming, "No move! No move!" He didn't have to tell me not to move.

Larry called Dr. Evans on the cell phone, describing the situation. He then told Achu to apply a poultice of crushed medicinal leaves combined with a special oil that would dull the pain, and then bring me in as soon as possible.

"How far away are you?" asked Dr. Evans.

"About an hour."

"We'll make preparations for surgery."

Larry had tears in his eyes as he picked me up and carried me toward the Rover, after a splint was made to hold my foot steady.

He gently held me close to him and as my arms went around his neck he whispered, "Oh, Baby, I'm so sorry. I can't bear to see you in pain." Then he kissed me gently and tenderly on the lips.

He had never called me "Baby," and he had never kissed me.

If I had any doubts of Larry's feelings for me they disappeared at that moment. We had talked very little of personal matters. When we were in the bush, all of us were concentrating on our work. At the end of the day Larry sometimes came to my tent to discuss the progress of our endeavors and whether or not any improvement could be made. Both of us were satisfied that we were accomplishing what we had set out to do.

One evening, during a lull in our conversation, I asked about his children. "What about Jason and Ruth? What are their interests and what are they studying?"

"Ruth plans to be a concert pianist and is completely absorbed in music. Jason is following in his mother's footsteps and is studying architecture."

We were near the Rover now; in fact, it was in sight. I knew Larry was getting tired. I was growing limp from one of the medicinal leaves Achu told me to chew, as it was a mild sedative.

As we drove up, everyone at camp rushed to meet us with a stretcher for me. My foot and ankle were x-rayed to determine the extent of damage, and then the nurse anesthetized me.

Before I went under, Larry said, "Lilly, you're going to be fine. I'll be here when you wake up."

The last figures I saw were Achu and Lomin, their brown bodies dripping with sweat and tears running down their faces. Their compassion touched my heart as nothing I had ever experienced.

I was confined to the Lodge for ten days on crutches with a cast covering my foot and extending to my knee. I worried that my accident might delay our project, but no one complained, at least not to my knowledge.

Larry and I used the time to edit and plan the best way to end the documentary. Eric and Paul (or Apollo, as he was sometimes called) worked on their equipment. Achu and Lomin went home for a few days. Lomin's wife was expecting a baby.

Finally, the men became restless and decided to scout new locations for our next filming. Several times they ran into the construction trucks resulting in confrontations.

Corrupt government officials had given big companies permission to cut down the trees and plants, destroying the rain forests.

In spite of efforts by honest officials to prevent this from happening, the rape of the land continued, and the only way we could help was going to be through showing our documentary to the world. This was our aim and hope.

After ten days, Dr. Evans said I could ride to a nearby site where we had planned to film. Larry carried me to a somewhat comfortable place to sit, and we debated as to whether or not the camera should show my cast. We decided to tell about the accident in the audio and show the cast.

Everything went well in the weeks that followed, but it was decided that we would need to stay two weeks longer than previously scheduled.

We were pleased with our work, and, with only three weeks left, were looking forward to going home and to getting the documentary ready for publication.

One day near noon, when we stopped to have lunch, Larry suddenly said, "I feel a migraine headache coming."

He had told me on the plane that he was subject to migraines, usually one or two a year, but he hoped he could get back home from this trip without suffering from one. He carried medication at all times, but still the attacks were so severe that bed rest and complete quiet were necessary for three or four days. In the past, he had been hospitalized at times.

Larry took the medication and said we should head back to the Lodge. By the time we arrived he was in terrible pain, so the nurse put him to bed. Two nurses were the only ones there, as the doctors had been called to a remote village because of an outbreak of malaria.

Three patients were in the infirmary and Alicia, the nurse, said that Larry should go to his room so that the other patients wouldn't bother him.

I said, "Tell me what to do, and I'll take care of him."

She handed me two bottles of pills. "This one, the pink one, is to be given every two hours; the green one every four hours. Bathe his face, head, neck and shoulders with cool water. Keep him quiet and don't talk."

Larry was also sick to his stomach, so Alicia decided to put him on an IV and an anti-nausea pill. I set the alarm in case I fell asleep, as the medications had to be taken at certain intervals. This strong, beautiful man looked so helpless. I felt so sorry for him, and without realizing it, I leaned over his bed and whispered, "Oh, Baby, I'm so sorry you're sick."

He reached for my hand and said, "Stay with me." I think he knew I would.

There's a saying, "Love is something you go through with someone." Larry and I had been through so much together during the time we were in this strange world far from home. We had bonded in a way we weren't even aware of—a bond that would last a lifetime.

I administered his medicine during the night and bathed his face, neck and shoulders with cool water. I said nothing. He dozed from time to time, and I was able to get in a few naps.

On the fifth day Larry had completely recovered, and I laughingly told him, "You're on your own now." He looked at me differently than before, and I wondered what he was thinking.

The last weeks flew by as we finished our projects. Now it was time to go home and get our film into the hands of the producer. Larry's friend, Tony Saunders, had agreed to do this. I had not met Tony, yet.

The day before we were to leave, Larry said, "Come walk with me."

It was late afternoon, a beautiful time of day in that part of the world. Base camp was situated on one and a half acres, and we walked through the vegetable garden to the northwest corner where orchids were hanging from the trees and bromeliads were attached in clusters to several trees.

It was a bittersweet moment. We had grown to love this land and its people. The project had made a profound impact on me, and a deep respect and admiration had developed for Larry. I felt an affinity never before experienced with anyone else.

We walked in silence for awhile. He stopped, took my hand and said, "Lilly, I think you know I love you."

I freed my hand and turned away in tears, trembling. He held me in his arms whispering, "It's all right to cry, Baby." Through tear-dimmed eyes and choking voice, I replied, "I love you, too, Larry."

For a moment the earth stopped spinning on its axis, time stood still. All I could feel was the pounding of my heart as we shared a lover's kiss.

Somehow I regained my composure. "We can't do anything about this, Larry, I have too much respect for Teresa, your children, you and myself. We have to let go."

"I agree, and I love you all the more for your moral stand."

In silence, hand in hand, we walked back to the Lodge.

"Goodnight, Larry."

"Goodnight, Lilly."

In spite of the emotional drain, I slept soundly.

Good-byes are always difficult, and this one was particularly sad. The helicopter that would take us to the airfield was already on the ground. Paul and Eric were on board. Achu and Lomin were there with their families—they had gifts for us and it was impossible to keep back the tears. The little children were so precious. These people of different backgrounds and cultures had forever won a place in my heart. We waved a final goodbye just before the door to the copter closed. I couldn't refrain from thinking a chapter of my life had closed also.

I think Larry and I both knew it was time to file our feelings in their proper place and concentrate on our partnership and work for the cause of "Protect the Earth."

We were anxious to get our documentary in production so that the entire world would be aware of the danger to our civilization.

Chapter 2

It was good to get home and three days after our return we had an appointment with the producer, Tony Saunders.

It never occurred to me to wonder what Tony would look like or be like. I had met many men in my life—I was surrounded by them at the university—but I did not see or meet anyone I thought was romantic. However, you know the saying, "You can't always tell a book by its cover."

Long ago I decided that women were more romantic than men, and I let it go at that. So I was totally unprepared as we entered Tony's office.

The door was open and he was sitting on the edge of his desk, one foot on the floor. His hand was resting on his knee.

His hair was dark brown, you might say black, slightly graying, high forehead. He was talking with a friend who was there to view our documentary.

"Larry, it's wonderful to see you. It's been a long time."

"Yes, it has been—so good to see you, Tony." Reaching for my hand, he said, "This is Lilly."

Then I saw his eyes—brown but not dark, medium brown maybe, mixed with greenish hazel, if there is such a thing. Absolutely the most beautiful eyes I had ever seen, and long lashes that no man should have. His lips were full but not excessively. I dislike a man with thin lips. Don't ask me why.

He stood up. He appeared to be 6'1" or 6'2"—well built, muscular. Wow! Another beautiful man and so unexpected.

Then I remembered my mother's saying, "Beauty is only skin deep, and beauty is in the eye of the beholder."

Tony extended his hand. "I've been anxious to meet you and see the documentary you and Larry made."

"Yes, I've been looking forward to this meeting also."

I wasn't sure what I was saying. Tony was single. Larry told me coming back on the plane that he had been married twice. Frankly, I didn't pay much attention. Now, it was a different story. I wanted to know everything about him.

I realized it was time to get on with my life. I knew where things stood with Larry, and I was confident we could work together as close friends and leave it at that.

It was time to set aside my personal feelings. We had an important documentary to present to the world.

Tony was impressed and enthusiastic with our work and the next several days we burned the midnight oil applying the final touches.

Finally, it was finished and Larry said, "I think it's time to celebrate." Teresa was back from her latest trip and Larry suggested the four of us go to dinner the following night.

"Oh," I thought, "what shall I wear?" A typical reaction as a woman.

I hadn't given much thought to clothes lately. Jungle attire was all I had worn in the past several months.

Maybe I would have time to go shopping. I must make time. Tony picked me up and we met Larry and Teresa at Lorenzo's, one of the best places to go for dinner and dancing.

This was the first time Tony and I had been alone and I was very nervous. He apparently sensed my uneasiness and said, "Now, we'll have an opportunity to learn more about one another."

"Yes."

"Your dress is lovely and you look beautiful."

"Thanks. It's new. I'm low on clothes. I haven't bought anything since returning from the other side of the world."

Larry and Teresa had reserved a table and were waiting for us.

"I've taken the liberty to order the wine."

My knowledge of fine wine was limited, so I said, "Good."

This was the second time I had met Teresa and only briefly when she was preparing for a trip. I liked her and she and Larry seemed very compatible as much as I hated to admit it.

Tony was looking at me in a different way from when we were working together. I felt flushed and was sure my face was red, much to my embarrassment. If anyone noticed they didn't say anything. Thankfully.

The wine was delicious and we toasted to the success of our project.

Tony kept looking at me and seemed hesitant. Then he said, "Would you like to dance?"

"It's been a long time and I don't dance very well."

"I haven't danced in awhile either so we'll struggle together."

I was ashamed of my thoughts. I was anxious to be in his arms and struggling sounded like fun.

Tony's lead was firm and smooth. I was surprised how easy it was to follow. No struggle this time. The music was big band tunes, my favorite. Before I realized it he was getting closer and closer until we were dancing cheek to cheek.

We danced through several numbers when Tony said, "Lilly, I'm starving. Let's eat."

"Yes, we did come for dinner." I almost forgot.

It was late when we got to my door. I knew Tony wanted to come in but I said, "It has been a wonderful evening, Tony, but I must get up early and report to the university. I may not have a job. They have been lenient with me and I need to find out how I stand."

He didn't say anything but got closer. I knew what was going to happen and I didn't know what to do about it.

At first I thought it was only going to be a hug but his lips were soon touching mine in a gentle, soft yet passionate kiss. I responded but slowly backed away at the same time he did.

"Goodnight, Lilly."

"Goodnight, Tony."

I didn't close the door immediately but watched as he walked toward the elevator. He turned suddenly.

"This is just the beginning, Lilly." Then he was gone.

The university extended my leave so I could write "Protect the

Earth" books for young people and children. The writing was easy, as I already knew what I wanted to say. I had several ideas on how to approach teens in an appealing manner.

I wrote during the day and went out with Tony most evenings. He planned interesting and fun things to do. Sometimes we went for long drives, sometimes we walked barefoot on the beach. Both of us were comfortable with little conversation.

The chemistry was slowly building and I knew it was close to the boiling point. One late afternoon was particularly torrid. We were having dinner at a casual restaurant overlooking the ocean. It was near sunset—so beautiful—so romantic. We were dancing to soft music and after a long silence he whispered, "I want you. I want you to be my woman. I want to be your lover. It's torture to be near you and not be able to touch you the way I want to."

My heart was pounding. Blood was rushing to my head and neck. I was breathing hard.

"I know, Tony, I know."

We walked outside to the porch and sat in a swing.

"What are we going to do, Lilly? I don't want to wait any longer."

Somehow I knew it was imperative to gain composure and try to think rationally. I had been raised in a very conservative southern environment with strict moral values, one of which emphasized the importance of celibacy until marriage. I was also taught to weigh matters and figure them out for myself. Therefore, I had remained a virgin until marriage. Looking back, I don't remember ever being tempted, for some strange reason.

After my husband Matt's death, I didn't date but plunged myself into my writing and after six months decided to go west. When I had the opportunity to join the faculty at the university I was happy to start a new life but not many social activities.

I got along well with men in my work keeping myself at a distance in regard to dating.

The day I met Larry something happened. I was attracted to him but set the feeling aside when I found out he was married. I came to the conclusion that perhaps it was destined for me to make life's journey alone, unencumbered.

Then Tony came along and things changed. He awakened feelings within me that I never knew existed. How could anyone remain celibate in a situation like this?

But was I ready for this? We had known each other for two and a half months. If we slept together, things would never be the same but I knew we couldn't continue the ways things were—too steamy.

"Tony, I feel the same way you do. The first day we met I was strongly attracted to you, but I don't think the time is right. If we will be patient, we'll know when the time is perfect."

"I respect you, Lilly, and I'll go along with your wishes. I just hope it will be soon."

"It will be, Tony. It will be."

I initiated a passionate kiss like never before.

I was afraid that the days to follow would be awkward but that was not the case. Tony was kind and considerate realizing I needed time and space.

One day he called me at my office. "I have to go to San Diego for three or four days, maybe a week. The officials at the zoo want to do a short subject film on tigers. I have agreed to direct and produce it."

"How interesting! I have always thought if I had to be an animal I would want to be a tiger."

"They are a magnificent and fascinating animal. I'm looking forward to doing this project."

Silence. Finally, I said, "I'll miss you, Tony. When are you leaving?"

"This afternoon. I'll miss you, too. I'll call."

He hung up before I had time to get emotional. I was glad.

My office was located on the fifth floor. Large windows overlooked a beautiful portion of the campus. The ocean was not in view but many times I thought I heard the waves coming ashore murmuring in rhythm, "Come with me. Come with me."

As I stood looking out, Ted entered the room. He was one of my associates in the Family Relations Department, and we spent many hours together discussing the various concepts regarding the correlation between men and women.

Ted was 35. His beautiful young wife died a year ago in childbirth. Their baby boy didn't survive either.

Ted was very intelligent and wise beyond his years. He understood human nature more completely than anyone I have ever known.

"Lilly, are you all right? You appear to be detached and far away."

"I'm confused, Ted. Why do I think I can write and lecture on the male-female connection? I'm kidding myself. I don't know the first thing. I can relate in the abstract but personally I'm a mess."

"Nonsense, Lilly. You have a very rare depth and insight. You're selling yourself short. What brought on this inaccurate evaluation? If this is too personal, I withdraw the question."

Ted knew I was dating Tony. They met briefly when Larry and Tony came to my office while we were working on "Protect the Earth."

Several times over morning coffee I told Ted how much I enjoyed being with Tony.

"I feel alive for the first time in a long while. I feel so comfortable when I'm with him. We don't have to talk all the time. We seem to be in tune with silence."

I wasn't ready to tell Ted everything at this point but I think he suspected more than I realized.

"Lilly, don't rush into this. Sometimes we get carried away by our emotions. I think you and Tony need to know one another better. Time will tell if you're right for each other."

As he spoke, a great phrase came to mind from *The Sound of Music*,— "Follow every rainbow until you find your dream."

"You know I'm here for you if you want to talk more."

"Thanks, Ted, you're a real friend."

Chapter 3

The two books for the younger generation were almost ready to be printed except for illustrations. Larry and I agreed that the right kind of artwork would be almost as effective as the words.

We talked with several local artists and visited art galleries but so far we were unsuccessful in finding what we were looking for.

I thought I would recognize what I had in mind—children with special expressions different from the ordinary.

Tony had been gone four days. He called and said everything was progressing well and he sounded enthusiastic but it would be four or five more days before he would be home.

He asked about my work. "We haven't been able to find an artist yet. I'm beginning to think maybe I expect too much."

"I'm confident you'll find exactly what you want. Just be patient."

"I hope so."

Several days later as I was leaving my classroom, Phil from the art department was standing in the hall waiting for me.

"Hi, Lilly, I have something you might be interested in."

He was holding the latest issue of a regional art magazine. "Read this ad."

It was advertising an art show being held in another part of the city, an area unfamiliar to me. It read, "Lesser known regional artists showing recent works on different subjects including children and old people."

"What do you think, Lilly?"

"I think it's worth a try. Thanks, Phil."

I called Larry but he wasn't in. I left a message: "I'm going to 416 Channel Street to an art exhibit."

The city map was in the car. Channel Street was north of the city on the waterfront—not the best part of town. I didn't want to go alone but felt the urgency to see this showing.

After several wrong turns, I finally reached Channel Street. It took forty-five minutes more to find No. 416. Several unsavory looking characters were on the street.

Ah, at last! The building needed a paint job and was in general disrepair. The place was apparently a haven for starving artists.

I parked in front, careful to lock the car, and headed for the door. The inside looked a little better—in fact, quite a bit better. The paintings were displayed well with proper lighting and I was impressed.

Several people were milling around not talking. There was an unusual quietness although I heard very soft music in the background. I looked for a program or brochure but didn't find it.

No one approached me so I decided to look on my own. It was a larger show than I expected so I followed the numbers. I was immediately impressed by the quality of work, although I'm not an authority.

About midway through the exhibit I came to paintings of children. It was evident that this was a different artist. Then I spotted the most fascinating picture I had ever seen. This is it!—five children of various ages playing on the seashore, their features and expressions exactly what I was looking for.

I stood several minutes engrossed and spellbound when a man spoke, "You must really like this one. I've watched you for awhile."

"Yes, are you the artist?"

"No, I don't know him. His work was brought in by a friend."

I moved on to the next painting by the same artist—children in a tree house; another one was children dancing in a field of flowers; older children feeding horses near a barn; the last one, two small girls playing with three kittens on the porch of a farm house. Nearby a boy was lying on the grass looking up as if day dreaming, a dog asleep by his side.

I was spellbound! This was exactly what I had dreamed of but never expected to find. I was speechless.

The man spoke again, "I'm Jack Longley, the curator."

"I have to locate this artist."

I began explaining briefly the reason I was so interested in these particular paintings.

"Unfortunately, I have very little information. Will Jenkins, who brings his work in from time to time, brought these the last time he came. We were very busy at the time and Will left before I could talk with him."

"Do you have an address or do you know anyone who is acquainted with him?"

"No, I don't. I'm sorry."

The phone in my purse rang. It was Larry.

"Where in the world are you?"

"I'm at the art exhibit on Channel Street. Can you meet me here? I've found the perfect paintings. I'll explain more when you get here."

"It may take forty-five minutes or more. What's that number again?"

"416."

Jack was looking in the right-hand corner of the paintings where all artists sign their work.

"Look at this Mrs…Miss…"

"Just call me Lilly."

In the right-hand corner was a small cross and the letter "C."

"What do you make of this?" I asked.

"I don't know, but I'll ask around and eventually we'll find this man, but it may take a while."

While waiting for Larry I studied the five paintings over and over again, each time discovering more substance and beauty.

"There you are." Larry came running in the door. I grabbed his hand and led him to the first painting, anxious to see his reaction. He studied each one carefully before saying anything.

"You're right, Lilly, they're perfect."

Jack came up and I introduced Larry. Jack gave a rather bleak account of the situation but insisted he would do everything possible to locate the mysterious artist.

In the weeks that followed we tried to concentrate on other things. Larry was busy at his job with "Protect the Earth" and I went back to the university to participate in a seminar I promised to do.

And then there was Tony. I was so glad to see him. I didn't realize how much I had missed him until I saw him coming toward me wearing that rather shy, mischievous grin.

We were dating two or three times a week depending on how busy we were. We didn't mention our previous conversation. Tony and I enjoyed many of the same activities so there was never a dispute about where, when, or what we would do.

One weekend he said, "I want you to take a trip with me next week."

"Oh?"

"My cousin lives 200 miles from here in the mountains. I talked with him recently and he invited us to visit."

"You've never mentioned a cousin. Tell me more."

"Henry is my first cousin. His father and my father were brothers. We grew up together and were very close. We often discussed what we would do in life. Henry wanted to stay in the mountains. He often said, 'I want a large log house near a stream.' I would say, 'How are you going to make a living?' He would reply 'I haven't figured that out.'

"As wonderful as life was there I wanted something different. I want to live in the city with the hustle and bustle of the business world. I want to be in the middle of the teeming millions."

"Not me, Tony, you can have the city."

"After high school, I entered the Pacific Southwest University and studied drama, took acting lessons and business management. Henry enrolled in an agricultural college and became interested in plant life and herbs growing in the mountains."

"And now?" I asked.

"Henry married his childhood sweetheart, Nell, and they live in a big log house with a porch running across the front. Oh, yes, it is situated near a river.

"They have two grown children, Alan and Rachel. Henry does

organic farming. Several years ago the government gave him a grant to research mountain herbs. He has a very impressive and interesting laboratory. Alan works with his father. Rachel married recently and lives nearby. In fact, I haven't met her husband."

I was fascinated by the story and wanted to meet them.

"Yes, Tony, I want to go with you. I can hardly wait, but first I want you to go with me to the art gallery on Channel Street and see the paintings I told you about."

"Yes, of course, when do you want to go?"

The next morning, I called Jack. "Jack, I want to bring a friend to see the paintings. Will you be there this afternoon?"

"Yes. Unfortunately, I have no news regarding our mysterious artist."

Tony was intrigued by the simplicity yet uniqueness of the paintings and studied them in detail. I pointed out the signature and he asked for a magnifying glass.

The markings appeared more distinguishable on two of the paintings.

"Look at this," he said.

As I leaned closer he pointed out something we had missed before. Underneath the "C," barely visible, were the letters "S-H."

"Jack, what can this mean?"

"I haven't the faintest idea."

"Could this be the initials of the painter or does it refer to a geographical location?" This was my first thought.

"Maybe," I said, "this is San something or Saint something."

"I'm afraid we're still at a dead end," Jack said.

"No, I don't think so," Tony replied. "I believe the S-H will prove to be a key leading to this man or woman."

By the time we left the gallery I was crying. Of course, this upset Tony. In the meantime the book was on hold until we could find illustrations.

It's always frustrating when you feel completely helpless in a situation but I thought to myself, "I can't allow this to get to me."

Two days later we were on the way to Henry's house. During the drive Tony told me more about his childhood and youth and I was able to see him in a different perspective.

I was anxious to meet Tony's relatives and the time passed quickly as Tony talked enthusiastically. I recognized the house from his description—a more beautiful scene I could never imagine.

As we approached the door a black Labrador roused from sleeping. The calmness and serenity had a profound effect on me. This was surely a place to shed your cares and troubles.

The door opened and a tall pretty woman came down the steps. "That's Nell."

She waved and I knew immediately I would like her. She hugged both of us and I felt at home.

"Henry and Alan are at the lab. I'll call them."

She pointed to a building at the side and back.

Henry was as warm and friendly as Tony had said.

"This is Lilly," Tony introduced me.

"We've been anxious to meet you. Naturally, we are curious about the woman he's bringing to meet his relatives."

I'm sure I was blushing but Tony took my hand, giving me a reassuring kiss on the cheek.

Alan was a bit shy. He was twenty and a student at a nearby small college. He was studying the environment—a subject dear to me so I knew we had a common interest.

Rachel and her husband, Grant Morgan, did not join us for dinner as they had a prior commitment. They lived about ten miles away and Grant taught at the college Alan attends.

After dinner or more correctly called supper in this case, Henry and Tony went outside. I wanted to help Nell clean up but she insisted that she and Alan would take care of it.

"Lilly, you and I will get acquainted tomorrow. Join the men on the porch. It's a lovely evening."

I don't like to interrupt men when they are deep in conversation so I stood hesitantly in the doorway.

Henry said, "Come out, Lilly, we have a full moon tonight."

"I don't want to interrupt."

"No, you're not."

Henry asked about my work. Tony had told him some of the details of the project including our search for the missing artist.

"I'm intrigued and impressed. Keep me informed. Alan and I are also concerned about the destructive forces endangering our world."

At this point, Henry said he needed to finish at the lab and would see us in the morning. Tony and I stood in silence holding hands, drinking in the beauty of the evening.

We became aware of soft music and looking through the window we saw Henry and Nell dancing.

"Nell has always liked to dance. I guess she persuaded Henry to go a few rounds before he goes to the lab. Shall we?"

No words were necessary and we danced a long time.

We were cheek to cheek only a breath apart. His strong arms made me feel so secure, so loved. In this different element among his relatives I was experiencing another side of Tony, and I liked it.

He whispered, "You know how I feel about you. I can't imagine life without you at my side. Up to now life's journey has been lonely and incomplete. I want us to journey together."

I knew of no appropriate words. My answer was a long, passionate kiss which I think took him by surprise.

We danced until I became so sleepy I could hardly stand. After all, it had been an exciting day. He led me upstairs to my room.

"Goodnight, Lilly, I'll see you in the morning."

"Goodnight, Tony."

He closed the door. I managed to get undressed and I'm sure I was asleep by the time my head hit the pillow. I awoke the next morning to the wonderful aroma of coffee. Nell appeared at the door with a cup for me.

"Tony says you like a little cream."

"Yes, that's right."

"Henry is making breakfast—ham, scrambled eggs, biscuits."

"I'll shower and be down in a few minutes."

Nell said the men were planning our day. They wanted to go to the rodeo. My first thought was I didn't have appropriate clothes.

When I got to the kitchen Rachel and Grant were there. They wanted to go with us. Nell found blue jeans that fit me plus a white shirt and waist-length jacket. It was my first rodeo, and I was very excited. I was amazed at the bravery and expertise of the riders.

The next morning I woke up at five and couldn't go back to sleep, so I put a robe over my gown and tiptoed out the back door following a path to the river. Water held a special allure for me—water flowing over rocks, cascading falls, waves coming in from the ocean, rolling in and out, repeating the cycle constantly.

I sat on a rock a long time to think. Then I stood, enthralled by the thought of what it is and what it does. There is more water on earth than dry land and a large percent of our bodies is water. We can't live without water. Why is this so?

I lost track of time and didn't hear Tony as he approached.

"Lilly, what are you doing out here?"

"I couldn't sleep, and I've told you before that I have a special affinity toward water. I can't explain it. I'm drawn to it whenever I see a stream, river or ocean."

"We're going back to the house now. You're barefoot and cold. You're shaking."

No one was up when we got back to the house so we curled up together in a hammock with a blanket and fell asleep immediately.

Henry woke us up a few hours later.

"What in the world are you doing out here?"

"Lilly decided to take an early morning walk."

We let it go at that and Henry didn't ask anything else.

We had already stayed longer than we planned. Henry and Nell kept urging us to stay and as wonderful as the visit had been, we needed to get back to our work.

They had planned a square dance for the next night and persuaded us to stay for it.

Furniture was moved out of the large living room and den. Neighbors and musicians came from miles around.

Long tables were set up in the yard and everyone brought food. Entire families came, from the youngest toddler to old men and women with canes. It was one of the biggest social events of the year.

While I was dressing Nell said she needed to tell me something.

"One of Tony's old girlfriends may be here. She has never gotten over him so you may have to be assertive."

This news was somewhat disturbing but I thought I could handle it. It might be a test of my stamina and ability to outwit another person.

I dressed a little more provocatively than planned, not knowing what kind of woman I might be up against.

"Her name is Betty," said Nell, "and she's a blonde. She was divorced about a year ago."

"Does Tony know this?"

"I'm not sure but I'll alert him to be on guard with her. She's very bold."

People began to arrive by car and truckloads. I had never seen so much excitement. Tony was waiting for me on the porch.

"Wow! Lilly, you look beautiful. All the men will try to take you away from me."

"I doubt that but they won't stand a chance. The first time I saw you in your office sitting on the corner of the desk you got my attention and you've held it ever since."

He pulled me to him in a somewhat passionate embrace and we were kissing when a voice shouted:

"Tony! Tony! It's you! How nice to see you."

Guess who? "Blonde Betty."

"Hi, Betty. I want you to meet Lilly."

"Hi, Lilly," then immediately turning back toward Tony she said, "I'll expect a dance with you later."

Tony didn't reply. Taking my hand he said, "Maybe we could hide out by the river."

"I don't think so. Henry and Nell expect us to mix and mingle. Why don't you dance with Nell and also Rachel, as I don't know anything about square dancing. I'll be fine. I like to watch people."

Many people wanted to speak to Tony since they hadn't seen him in several years. Some of the older people had known him since he was a baby.

I was sitting with a group of children telling them stories from my books about bad people who wanted to cut down trees and flowers. I promised to send copies to their school when they were finished.

Tony walked up. "I'll have to dance with Betty or she won't leave me alone."

"Of course. I understand."

I watched as they danced. In square dancing you're not very close to your partner and I could tell she was trying to persuade him to leave the group. He was resisting and an argument was in progress. I didn't know what to do. Nell was thinking ahead of me. She told the musicians to play some tunes from the big band era and she told me, "Interrupt them. Grab Tony and say, 'Sorry, this is my dance.'"

Did I have the courage to do this? I didn't hesitate long and in a flash Tony and I were whirling across the room leaving a stunned Betty in an embarrassing situation. We kept dancing until we thought things had settled down. We wanted to appear to make light of the incident.

"Thanks, Lilly, for taking the matter in your own hands. I wasn't handling it very well."

"Actually, Nell took care of it. I just had to gather enough courage to interrupt."

Nell walked up and said that Betty left.

"I invited her to leave and told her she had always tried to cause trouble for Tony."

A man came up behind Tony and tapped him on the shoulder.

"It's been a long time since I have seen you, cousin."

"Bobby, you rascal, where did you come from?"

"I heard you were in the area."

"Lilly, this is Bobby Gray, first cousin on my mother's side. Our mothers were sisters. Bobby, this is Lilly."

"And where did you find this pretty woman?" Bobby asked, extending his hand.

Tony laughed. "I found her at the seashore. She's a sea nymph."

They apparently had lots of catching up to do so I excused myself and joined Nell and the other guests. Our visit was over and I was sad to leave. A few days ago I didn't know Tony's relatives and now I was in tears saying goodbye. We rode in silence. Words did not seem fitting. Nell had packed a lunch for us as we were late leaving and we didn't speak until Tony said he was hungry.

He remembered a nice place to stop and by the time we spread the food on a pretty cloth Nell had put in the basket, I was feeling better.

"Why did you tell Bobby I'm a sea nymph?"

"I guess because water appears to hold a certain magnetism for you and it just popped into my head."

"It's strange but I don't know myself why I'm drawn to water. I'll probably never know."

We relaxed for awhile on a blanket and I couldn't resist snuggling in the crook of Tony's arm. He didn't seem to mind.

It was late when we got back to the city and we had already decided I would stay the night at Tony's house, which was on the north side, rather than drive another thirty-five miles to my apartment on the south side.

The next morning during the drive to my apartment I told Tony how much I enjoyed the trip.

"I love your relatives, Tony. They made me feel welcome and at home. I admit I was a little apprehensive at first."

"I knew you would love them and they love you too. Nell told me to not let you get away."

"What are you doing today, Tony?"

"I'm behind on some projects and I need to check on some other things. What about you?"

"I'm going to call Larry. He may have heard from Jack. I hope he has some news."

"I'll call you tonight," he said as he hugged and kissed me. The kiss was somehow different. I felt the bond between us growing stronger. I wanted the moment to last but I knew there would be other moments even more wonderful.

Chapter 4

I phoned Larry. "Hi, Larry."

"Hi, Lilly, how was your trip?"

"Great. Tony's relatives are nice, friendly and very hospitable. Life there is quieter and slower paced. Have you heard from Jack?"

"He called to say there's nothing new but a woman who works part time at the gallery is very familiar with the area south of Seattle. She thinks the S-H is the name of a small town or fishing village that may not be on the map. She is going to keep looking."

I know I sounded disappointed.

"Lilly," Larry said, "I still think we'll find this artist. Jack says he heard Will Jenkins was in Italy. He goes every few years but always returns."

"It's so hard to be patient," I said.

"I know."

Time to unpack and settle down. I was sitting on the edge of the bed wondering what to do next, not wanting to do anything.

I decided to check in with the university. I still enjoyed my work there. There was something exciting about being a part of campus life.

As I walked from my car toward my office taking the longer walkway, I met many students. Some I knew; some I didn't. I always spoke and today I wondered what their lives would be like five or ten years from now.

I hoped they would reach their goals and find their dreams but I also knew there would be some failures. When I was their age I never imagined I would live on the west coast, teach personal relationships, become involved in international conservation, make a trip to the rain forest and, I smiled to myself, fall in love with two men.

Was this really me, Lilly Tompkins, a southern girl, who had led a rather mundane life?

Tony was swamped with work. He got behind while we were gone. A week passed during which time we talked by phone.

Just when I was feeling lonely and sorry for myself the phone rang.

"Hi, Lilly."

"Hi, Tony."

"What's wrong, you don't sound right?"

"I miss you, Tony."

"I miss you, too, and we're going to do something about it. Would you like to spend several days at my house? I want to cook for you and make my special dishes."

I've never been a person to be deceptive about my feelings or play hard to get. I'm very frank, maybe too much so at times. So I didn't hesitate.

"I would love to."

"Can you be ready by Thursday morning?"

It was Tuesday. "Yes, that will be fine."

Tony's house was beautiful, completely surrounded by a high brick wall covered in ivy. The entrance was through iron gates opened only by phone or electronic device. The drive leading to the house was lined with tropical plants and a few palms.

A lattice veranda ran the length of the house, which was covered with lilacs and roses. To the left and down the hill was the private beach on the ocean.

Facing the entry was a spiral staircase leading to a sitting room, den, and library combination. Three bedrooms and two baths radiated off this room. I had slept in one of these rooms the night we came back from our trip.

Downstairs to the left was an average sized dining room. Tony preferred entertaining small groups. This room led to a large kitchen and breakfast area, with windows overlooking a perfectly landscaped flower garden that ran the length of the back.

The living room in the center of the house extended from front to back with windows. To the right a hall led to the large master suite containing an entertainment area, television and musical equipment. Tony's grand piano was in the living room. He was a frustrated pianist playing mostly for therapy.

Adjoining the master suite was a smaller bedroom with a bath. Tony's bathroom was almost as big as my apartment.

Oh, yes, over the iron gates at the entrance was the word "Canaan." I thought it was a very fitting name for his home.

This was where I would spend the next several days with a man I had come to know and love.

"Lilly, you can have a room upstairs or the small room that joins mine."

When he invited me to his house he had said, "There are no strings attached."

"The small one next to yours will be fine."

Alexander and Josie took care of the house and grounds. They were a middle age couple who had worked for Tony ten years.

Josie was preparing lunch when we arrived and Alexander insisted on carrying my luggage.

After lunch Tony said, "I want to show you something. Let's go out the back door."

There was a driveway leading off to the right and a parked jeep. We rode about the length of a football field and came to more iron gates.

"Read the sign before I open the gates," Tony said.

"Welcome to the Promised Land."

"What in the world is this?" I asked

Tony was enjoying keeping me in suspense. "Close your eyes and wait until I say 'Open.' Open."

What a surprise! We were in the middle of a large vineyard—vines loaded with the most beautiful grapes I had ever seen.

I was speechless. Then I managed to say, "Tell me about it."

"This is my vineyard. It may appear large but it is small by most standards. We sell some of the grapes to a local winery but mostly

Josie makes jelly to sell at local stores."

Leaving the vineyard we came to a house.

"This is Alexander and Josie's house." It was beautiful and similar to Tony's but on a smaller scale.

"There's more."

On the other side of the house was an orchard—an orange grove, grapefruit trees, also peach and plum trees.

"This is amazing. I assume Alexander and Josie take care of this too."

"Yes, and at the back of their house is a vegetable garden. There is so much work at certain times they need help. Alexander's two nephews work part time."

"Tony, you're full of surprises. I didn't know about these things."

"One other thing—the winery we sell the grapes to produces a limited amount of wine under our copyright label "Promised Land Wine."

Tony said "we" as he considers Alexander and Josie partners.

"I would like to taste your wine and also visit the winery."

"And you will."

The sun was going down. From the kitchen windows I could see the waves coming ashore, going back out, coming ashore, going back out—perfect timing as if a director was waving a baton. I felt the pull of the water almost without control as I started to the beach. What power did water have over me, and why? The waves seemed to beckon me, whispering a love song with words I couldn't understand.

Tony followed me to the beach and was standing behind me. I turned and as he embraced me, kissing me in a way never before experienced, I realized this was the hour, the time had come. Tony knew, too. No words were necessary.

I unbuttoned his shirt and removed it. He opened the neck of my dress and it fell in the sand. The sun sank into the horizon and the earth stood still. The only sound was the water as it rolled ashore.

I put my hand on his chest and felt his heart beat. As he hesitated I took his hand and placed it on my breast so he could feel my heart beat. There was no doubt. They were beating as one.

It was time for us to be one in the complete and inexorable way when a man loves a woman and a woman loves a man.

This was the way it was meant to be—in the beauty of the early evening as the full moon made its appearance.

The waves provided a crescendo that sealed the bond that would never be broken. We knew we would never be the same.

The next few days were beyond description. Tony and I were in a state of ecstasy. We looked at each other in a different way. We now felt free to touch without restraint. It was wonderful.

Alexander and Josie discreetly kept their distance and worked in their garden and the vineyard.

Early one morning, Tony said, "Lilly, have you ever seen the wine country, the hundreds of acres of vineyards?"

"No, I haven't."

"Would you like to go today?"

"Oh, yes."

I knew Tony owned a small plane and had a pilot's license but I had never flown with him.

He decided to let Walter, an employee at the hangar, pilot so he could point out the scenery.

It was breathtaking, as far as the eye could see. I had seen grapevines but nothing compared to this. The magnitude was overwhelming.

"Later, we'll take a helicopter so you can get a closer look."

I thought how truly blessed we are in this country—the rich abundance we enjoy and often take for granted. What a contrast to the devastated land in other countries! That was something I had seen firsthand.

I mentioned this to Tony.

"Yes, we often take for granted this land of plenty, but Lilly, you're trying to do something about the problem elsewhere in the world."

"Sometimes I get discouraged with my feeble efforts but after seeing this and being reminded of the richness of our land, I'm more determined than ever to help educate the younger generation particularly of the need to 'Protect the Earth.'"

These were my thoughts as I prepared for bed that night. I kept my clothes in the closets of the small bedroom and used the bath there, but I now slept with Tony in his super king sized bed.

When I entered his room it was aglow with at least a dozen candles, all sizes, shapes and colors. Flowers were everywhere, and the satin sheet was covered in rose petals.

He stood beside me—this well-built, muscular beautiful man. I looked deep into his eyes and I saw the kindest, most caring and gentle man I had ever known. For the first time in my life, I felt fulfilled and loved in the way every woman has a right to feel but perhaps few have found.

I fell asleep in Tony's arms, safe, and secure with the knowledge that I was the most fortunate woman in the world.

I kept my apartment in the city but spent the weekends at Tony's house. Although I was happier than ever I sometimes had guilty feelings. I believed and still do believe that sex before marriage is wrong; this is what I taught the people in my classes at the university and yet I also believe there are gray areas in almost all situations.

I rationalized that Tony and I were older; both of us had been married before. It was not the lust of youth when hormones are raging out of control with only one thought—instant gratification—but rather the desire for oneness equally shared that comes with maturity.

In my counseling sessions with couples I found many interesting facts. Some couples reported they were glad they had lived together prior to marriage as it gave them an opportunity to know and understand each other. They were able to communicate better; masks came off, the veneer peeled away and pretense removed.

A few couples said they wished they had lived together first. They felt adjustments would have been easier. Several were having trouble in their marriages and even thinking about divorce. None of these situations was proof of one theory or another.

Our culture still frowns on this lifestyle. We know that marriage is the basis and foundation for the home. Nevertheless I wasn't ashamed of my love for Tony and I knew we would marry at the proper time.

We went for long drives and walks on the beach, often not talking. We were content to hold hands and be near each other with our own special means of communication. Also we spent time with Josie and Alexander. The only thing I knew about them was that they were of Polynesian and French descent.

One morning while Josie was cleaning she said, "Alexander and I would like you and Tony to have dinner with us tonight if you don't have plans. Alexander wants to prepare some special recipes from the islands."

"That would be wonderful."

"We'll tell you about our families and how we came to be in the States."

"How interesting."

People are fascinating to me and I'm always eager to learn about different backgrounds and cultures. That night as we followed the path and went through the gateway to the vineyard the aroma of grapes was tantalizing. We stopped to sample a few.

"Tony, do you think grape vines were in the Garden of Eden?"

"Absolutely. That area where the Tigris and Euphrates Rivers merge was rich in grapes and tropical fruit."

"Now I know," I said, "the reason for naming your house and grounds Canaan—the Promised Land."

As we got closer to the house another delicious smell was in the air. Josie met us at the front door.

"Alexander is in the back grilling Polynesian pork."

Tony joined him while I went inside with Josie. The house was lovely. The decor was tropical—very bright colors with unusual fabrics and tastefully done. It was a place that made you feel cheerful and happy. Soft Hawaiian music in the background, delicious food, and the beautiful table setting provided a perfect island atmosphere.

Already it had been a very special evening and then Alexander said, "I want to tell you about my family. My grandparents left the Fiji Islands when my father was ten and his sister was eight. The economy had deteriorated and many people were leaving and going to California. They became migrant workers in the fields and vineyards.

"When my father and his sister finished high school they entered college due to the benevolence of a mission program for the children of migrant workers. In college he met my mother who was born in California but whose parents came from the islands in the same general area where my grandparents had lived.

"My father majored in engineering and upon graduation married the girl who would be my mother. She became a teacher. So I grew up in a home that emphasized education.

"I started with engineering but soon found out it was not for me. I tried other fields but nothing suited me until one day I visited a large nursery. I applied for a job and liked it. I dropped out of college, which brought sadness to my parents.

"The nursery did landscaping commercially and residentially, planting fruit trees and vineyards. I had found my calling and was determined to learn everything about growing fruits and vegetables. I also wanted to learn the art of landscaping."

When we finished dinner it was decided we would hold dessert until later. I was glad we had waited to taste Josie's delicious island recipe. It consisted of a layer of thin flaky crust topped with fresh tropical fruit. A sauce different from any I had ever tasted was poured on top and the finishing touch was a dollop of whipped cream. Freshly brewed coffee made it even more delectable.

Now it was time to hear Josie's story.

"My great grandparents lived in Hawaii. My great grandfather was Dutch and my great grandmother was French. They had two sons and two daughters. The youngest daughter was my grandmother. Her name was Elise. She married her high school sweetheart when they were both eighteen. Luke Lee was a native Hawaiian and they decided to come to southern California to seek their fame and fortune.

"Elise and Luke Lee had one son and three daughters. The son was my father, Horace. All of my forefathers were furniture makers and designers. My grandfather and father worked in a furniture factory but hoped to have their own business, which they did eventually.

"My father attended a trade school and also took classes at a small junior college. The manager of the factory noticed the excellent workmanship displayed by my father and complimented him.

"One day he said, 'Horace, do you have a girlfriend?'

"'No, I don't,' was his reply.

"'Well, I have a daughter you might be interested in. Would you consider having dinner with my family some evening?'

"What do you do when your boss asks you to meet his daughter? He valued his job and although very skeptical he agreed.

"But he was in for a surprise. She was very beautiful but extremely shy. It was love at first sight for both of them. Her name was Rosa Lee. They were married six months later. They had three children. I'm the oldest. I have a brother and a sister."

It appeared that Josie was about to complete her story. I spoke up, "But Josie you haven't told us how you met Alexander."

"Oh, yes. I was working part time at a florist while attending college and Alexander was working at the nursery where we bought some of our plants. I met him when he made the deliveries.

"I thought he was attractive and I tried to make our conversations last as long as possible. However, although he was cordial he didn't seem interested. I was determined to capture this man."

Alexander spoke up and said, "I was trying to play hard to get." He was smiling as he said it.

Several weeks passed and then one day just as Tony and I were coming in from a walk the phone rang. Josie answered it. "It's for you, Lilly."

It was Larry. "Our artist has been located."

I was very excited. "Where, when and how?"

"Will Jenkins had been in Italy and came in the gallery two days ago. He did not plan to be so long but met several artists and they decided to travel through the countryside.

"Our mysterious artist's name is Cecil, pronounced 'Sethul' rather than Cecil. He lives in a small fishing village called Sea Haven."

"Where is Sea Haven?"

"About 15 miles south of Seattle on Puget Sound."

"When can we go?"

"Will is going to contact Cecil and tell him about us. I hope we can set up an appointment soon. When are you coming back to the city, Lilly?"

"I'll be back at my apartment on Monday."

It was ten days before we heard from Will. Cecil would welcome us any time. In fact, he was anxious to meet us since we were so interested in his paintings.

I was very excited but also sorry to leave Tony. Larry said we might be gone a week or ten days.

I was quite emotional by the time we got to the airport. When I kissed Tony, tears ran down my cheeks and I clung to him as long as possible.

Larry said, "Lilly, we have to board now."

He walked on ahead as I lingered.

"I have to go now, Tony."

I hurried away and Tony called to me, "Lilly, will you marry me?"

I kept going, looked back and said, "Yes, yes, yes."

When I reached the door of the plane I was crying audibly. The flight attendant said, "Are you all right?"

"Yes, I'm fine."

Larry was standing by our seats. He took one look at me and said, "What happened? What's wrong?"

"Tony asked me to marry him."

"And you're crying?"

"It was a surprise, totally unexpected."

Larry sensed I didn't want to talk for awhile and I continued crying softly. When he did speak he said, "Why did Tony decide to propose at this time?"

"I haven't the faintest idea."

That thought was on my mind, too, but it would have to wait until I could talk with Tony. In the meantime Larry and I needed to discuss our meeting with Cecil. What was he like? Would he be receptive to our proposal to do the illustrations for my book?

Chapter 5

Some time ago we decided to buy the paintings in the gallery. Jack had several customers who had shown interest and we were afraid they would be sold. Larry bought two, I bought two, and Tony bought one for his office. He wanted the one showing young people feeding horses near a barn. We didn't know what price Cecil would want but we were prepared to pay.

After we landed in Seattle we rented a car and now we were near our destination. A large body of water was in view, sails going up on a schooner and a number of small sailboats that looked like mammoth butterflies skimming across the water.

"Stop, Larry, I want to get out of the car."

A strange feeling came over me that I had been there before but I knew it wasn't possible. I told Larry and he said, "I've occasionally had similar feelings also, but they soon pass."

This was different. Water, natural bodies of water, held some kind of a mystical restraint on me that I couldn't explain. The beach at Tony's house gave me this same sensation. It was disturbing—I didn't know how to deal with it.

An old man and a young boy with a bucket and fishing poles walked up.

"Hi, where are you folks going?"

Larry answered, "We're looking for a village called Sea Haven."

"You're close. It's around the next turn. Who are you looking for?"

"Cecil, the artist. Do you know him?"

"Everybody knows Cecil. Sea Haven is a small community of not more than four or five hundred people who mostly make their living fishing. We're skeptical of strangers, as we don't get many visitors. We're off the beaten path."

"Cecil knows we're coming to see him. Will you tell us how to get to his house? Also we'll need a place to stay for a few days. Do you have a motel?"

"Nope. There's a boarding house called Ezra's Place. It's for men only. Fishermen stay there from time to time after being out on a schooner. The lady will have to stay somewhere else. Maybe Maudie will take her in," said the old man gesturing toward me.

"Who's Maudie?"

"An old woman who lives near the pier. She's kinda strange but harmless and a real good cook."

The man and the boy went on and said, "Good luck."

Larry and I looked at each other quizzically.

"What are we getting into, Larry?"

"I don't know, Lilly, but you and I made it through several months in the jungle. We can handle this."

Ezra had one room left and after Maudie gave me the third degree she agreed to take me in. She said it was only because we came to see Cecil.

The local diner was a fish, chips and ale place. We were almost at the door when a boy about twelve ran up and said Cecil wanted us to eat with him. It was apparent that everyone in the village knew we had come to see Cecil.

"Follow me," the boy said, "I'll take you to Cecil's house."

You didn't need a car in Sea Haven. Everything was condensed to the area around the harbor except for a few houses in the outlying areas.

So we followed the boy not knowing what to expect. At last we were going to meet the mysterious artist. He led us to a two-story building. The sign over the door of the lower half read, "Bill's General Store."

On the outside of the building were stairs leading to the upper level. The boy motioned for us to follow up the stairway.

When we reached the top a door opened and a man said, "Come in, I'm Cecil." He turned to the boy. "Good job, Joshua," and the boy disappeared as quickly as he had appeared.

"I'm Larry and this is Lilly."

"Welcome to my humble abode," he said as he gave us a hearty handshake.

We walked into a large open area that ran the length of the building which was living room, dining area and kitchen combined. The decor was in excellent taste.

As I stood taking it all in that strange feeling came over me again. "I've been here before," yet I knew I had never even been in the state of Washington.

"Your home is so warm and inviting. I almost feel that I've been here before," I said.

"Good, we want you to feel at home," Cecil said as he introduced us to a lovely young woman.

"This is Miriam. She has prepared our dinner. Everyone in Sea Haven eats fish every day prepared in different ways. Miriam is an excellent cook."

Cecil was not what I expected. He was younger than I pictured, probably in his mid-forties. His hair was dark, he had an immaculately groomed beard, and beautiful dark blue eyes.

Miriam was a friendly woman with a beautiful smile. She had long dark brown hair and brown eyes. I guessed her age in the early thirties.

"I hope dinner is to your liking. We don't get many visitors in Sea Haven so it is a pleasure to cook for you."

The fish was broiled, seasoned with herbs and spices served with brown rice. The green salad had an unusual dressing—delicious. Dessert was a fruit cobbler made of peaches, pears, and dark cherries.

The meal and the setting were totally different from what Larry and I had anticipated.

Larry waited for Cecil to open the conversation regarding the paintings.

"Larry, tell me about the project and the documentary on conservation. Will Jenkins knew very little so I'm anxious to hear about it."

Larry started at the beginning up to the point of seeing his paintings at Jack's Art Gallery.

"Lilly and I are very impressed with your work and would like for you to do the illustrations for the two books she has written. The aim of the books is to provide awareness of the serious condition of our earth."

"How many illustrations are we talking about?"

"Eight or ten at least."

I spoke up, "We should tell you we have bought the five paintings; that is, we have them in our possession."

"Jack told me he had released them to you."

"We need to discuss a purchase price with you," Larry said.

"I'll have to think about it."

It was getting late so I suggested we continue our discussion the next day.

I was up early the next morning and walked to the water's edge. I took off my shoes and was wading ankle deep when Maudie called me from her porch, "Time for breakfast. Hurry before it gets cold."

The feeling was driving me crazy. I couldn't explain it and I didn't know how to tell anyone except Larry. He took it lightly and brushed it off as nothing unusual. Maudie had fish, potatoes, scrambled eggs and homemade biscuits. I decided to forego the fish but the other food was very tasty.

I needed to call Tony but Maudie didn't have a phone. She said she was sure I could call from Cecil's place.

Miriam and Cecil were finishing coffee when we got there. I was curious about their relationship but didn't ask. Miriam excused herself saying she needed to buy groceries. Larry was bolder than I. "Miriam is a lovely woman." He hesitated and Cecil smiled knowingly.

"Yes, she is. She's my housekeeper, cook, best friend and good companion. We don't live together but we have discussed marriage. I'm twelve years older and I want her to be sure this is what she wants."

"How did you meet?"

"I met Miriam when I was teaching art in San Francisco. She was a student at the university and we kept running into one another so we developed a friendship. We had an unusual rapport from the start.

"I was getting tired of big city life and one summer five years ago I discovered Sea Haven while on vacation. It had a profound effect on me—so quaint, charming, slower paced, and I felt I had been here before."

I looked at Cecil in astonishment. "Cecil," I said, "I felt this same way when we got here yesterday. It's strange, isn't it?"

"It certainly is." I suddenly realized I needed to call Tony.

"Cecil, may I use your phone to call my fiancé?"

"Oh, I assumed you and Larry were married."

"No, we're good friends and business partners."

"I don't have a phone but you can use the one in the General Store downstairs."

"Hi, Tony."

"Hi, Lilly. I wondered when I would hear from you. I miss you."

"I miss you too. It's beautiful here, quaint and charming. Cecil is nice and friendly."

"Where are you calling from?"

"The General Store."

"Have any negotiations been made?"

"No, we haven't reached that point. I hope something works out today. I'll call you again in a day or two. I love you, Tony. I have to go now."

Larry and Cecil were motioning from upstairs.

"I'm sure you would like to see my studio."

A small stairway from the kitchen led to the garret. Windows lined the entire front and back. Blinds could be pulled so that adjustments could be made to correct the lighting.

"Come to the front windows, Lilly."

A large schooner was pulling away from the harbor and several small sailboats were raising their sails. I gasped. Cold chills ran over me. I know I've been here before, but no, I haven't. I couldn't.

"Incredible view, isn't it?"

"Yes."

Chapter 6

Artists are very fascinating. I like to look at their palettes filled with different colors, tints and hues, the various brushes that stroke the canvas bringing life to scenes of nature and people.

Cecil was talking, "After I talked with Will and I knew you were coming here, I started a painting. It isn't finished but I think you'll get the idea."

Off center was a large tree. Near the top a boy sat on a branch giving the appearance of his feet swinging. His look was complete confidence. Several branches below a girl was climbing up but looking back at the ground. She seemed unsure and apprehensive.

On the ground two very young children were playing in the dirt, completely oblivious to the ones in the tree.

I was speechless. Larry laughed. "When Lilly is speechless it means something has a profound effect on her."

"Oh, Cecil, it's perfect. This is the kind of illustrations we're looking for. When I saw your work at Jack's Gallery I told Larry we must find you."

"How soon do you want these pictures?"

I laughed. "Yesterday." Becoming serious I said, "We've waited this long for the perfect material so whatever time you need. Can you give us an estimated time frame? We would want reproductions of the paintings we have."

"It wouldn't take long to reproduce those and if you want five or six more I could probably have them ready in a month."

I couldn't resist hugging Cecil. "You cannot imagine what this means to me and to Larry."

"Now if you can stay a few more days and give me ideas for the others maybe I could sketch them in and you would know how the finished illustrations will look."

"Wonderful! We'll stay."

I was in a state of ecstasy and almost unbelief. We had waited so long for the perfect material.

"I'm going to browse through the General Store downstairs. What are you going to do, Larry?"

"I'm going to the Fish and Chips Diner and listen to the fishermen's tall tales as they sip their ale. I'll meet you back at the General Store."

A tour of the General Store was an education. I had never seen so much varied merchandise. Some items looked as if they belonged to a different century. I had no idea what some of the things were. Miriam walked in to pick up a few staples and she said, "What do you think?"

"It's overwhelming."

"If you're interested in unusual jewelry you should look in the display case. I'll see you tonight; you and Larry are coming to dinner?"

"Yes, thank you."

A nice looking older gentleman was at the counter. "Can I help you look for something in particular?"

"No, I'm just curious."

"You're the lady with the man visiting Cecil."

"Yes."

"We have several beautiful gems that are indigenous to this area. Some have been made into various pieces of jewelry. We also have an excellent craftsman who makes the stones into whatever you want."

"How interesting. Tell me about the blue stone that looks like a small earring."

"That's a very rare blue moonbeam gem and it's a man's earring. The blue moonbeam is found in the shell of a rare clam-like creature. They are only found at night and when there is a full moon. Researchers have tried to learn more about them but have been unable to do so. They have been located in the last ten years and only in this area."

The stone was beautiful, three shades of blue in small semi-circular design. I wondered if Tony would like it and if he would wear it. I thought it would look good on him but I didn't know whether or not he would wear an earring.

Larry wore a very small diamond in one ear. It's his birth stone and I think it is very attractive.

"How much?" I asked.

Without batting an eye he said, "$1500."

What a shock!

"I said it was a very rare gem."

"Let me think about it."

I was about to walk away when Larry came in.

"Have you found something you want, Lilly?"

I told him the story of the blue moonbeam and asked the man to show it to Larry.

"What do you think?"

"I like it; it's unique."

"But do you think Tony would like it? And it's $1500."

"Oh, wow!"

"If I take it," I said, addressing the man, "and my fiancé doesn't like it, may I return it next month?"

"I'll have to ask the boss."

A large, rough-looking man came up. "If Cecil will vouch for you, you may return it."

"I need to think about this. I'll decide before we leave."

I thought to myself, "I'll check with Cecil first."

I liked Maudie's house. It was plain, simple and perhaps meager by some standards. Also there was an indescribable charm about it. The next morning, as I had done before, I woke up early and headed for the shore.

There was a mist over the water and the fishing boats were barely visible in the early light of dawn. The sailboats were in their moorings, moving slightly as the waves came ashore, waiting for their owners to raise their sails.

Again, as many times before, the feeling came over me, the

sensation in the presence of moving waters. What to make of it? I know not.

Maudie joined me. "Come, sit on the porch and I'll tell you a story, some say a legend but I know it to be true. It's the story of the water baby."

"Sounds intriguing," I said.

"About thirty-five years ago, give or take a year or two, a young girl named Anna married a young fisherman. They made love on the beach, actually in the water, and she conceived. The couple was very happy and they looked forward to the birth of their child.

"In the seventh month of Anna's pregnancy Tom set out on a two or three day fishing trip. Anna kept busy with preparations for the baby and the time passed quickly. Tom did not come home the third day or the fourth and on the fifth day several schooners went in search of Tom.

"Every day Anna went to the water's edge gazing longingly into the vast expanse of sky and sea. Time passed and no sign of Tom or his boat was found.

"In the ninth month Anna was found at dawn on the beach. She had given birth to a baby girl almost in the water. She was alone but was all right."

"What a story! What happened after that?" I said.

"When the baby was three months old, Anna and the baby disappeared. No one knows where they went or what happened to them. Efforts to locate them were to no avail. No clues were left behind. Years went by with no word from Anna. Tom and his boat were never found. The village people talk about it to this day as the story of the water baby."

"How fascinating! And so strange that no one has heard anything through the years. It almost sounds like a tall tale the fishermen like to tell."

"I know but I believe it to be true."

It was time for me to meet Larry. We had an appointment with Cecil. I was anxious to see what he had done on the paintings. Too, I missed Tony and I was ready to go home.

Cecil had accomplished quite a bit and we were very pleased with the paintings so Larry and I decided to stay two more days, confident that Cecil could complete the work without us.

The next day I told Larry that I would like to go out on a schooner.

"Do you think it's possible?"

"I doubt it but we'll try."

We were told that women are not allowed on schooners. Fishermen thought it was bad luck but maybe someone with a sailboat would take us out.

A woman and her son who looked to be thirteen or fourteen were raising the sails on a boat and Larry called to them.

"Can we sail with you? We'll be glad to pay you."

"Sure, get in. My name is Laura and this is my son, Billy."

"I'm Larry and this is Lilly."

We were confident Laura knew us as everyone in the village did. It was a perfect day, wind just right, bright blue sky, soft billowing clouds floating by. They seemed to be waving to us.

As we stood facing the wind, my hair blowing in the breeze, Larry slipped his hand around my waist. I leaned my head back on his shoulder. This was the first we had touched since we talked in the garden at Base Camp in Kabouch. That seemed like years ago now and worlds apart, but for the moment we enjoyed a bittersweet interval of closeness and intimacy in complete innocence. We didn't speak. No words were necessary.

Billy was shy but I was sure he wanted to talk with us.

"Where do you go to school?" I asked.

"My mom home schools me. Once a month I get together with other students who are home schooled and we take field trips and do other neat things."

"What are you interested in, Billy?" Larry asked.

"Do you mean what do I want to do when I grow up?"

"That's right."

"I think I want to study oceanography."

Laura spoke up, "He has lots of books on the subject and living near so much water it seems natural to have this interest."

This was a wonderful opportunity for us to discuss the "Protect the Earth" project so Larry told Billy about the devastation taking place throughout the world that was affecting our ecological system. He related in detail our trip into the rain forest and the documentary we made.

"In fact," Larry said, "it is the reason for our visit with Cecil. Lilly has written two books for young people explaining what is happening to our world. We saw some of Cecil's paintings at an art gallery in Santa Barbara where we live and we came to ask Cecil if he would do paintings of children and young people to use as illustrations in the books."

Laura spoke up. "We heard that your visit here had something to do with conservation and we are very interested in the subject. We want to preserve our way of life in this area."

The wind had picked up and Billy was helping his mother maneuver the sails. This was my first time in a sailboat and I was enjoying every minute of it.

That evening was the last meal with Cecil and Miriam and I hated to leave. We had a special rapport with them. The paintings were beyond our expectations. Cecil said they would be ready in about a month so Larry and I decided to come back and get them. We didn't want to trust them to other means of transportation.

I still had not decided about the blue moonbeam earring so I mentioned it to Cecil, "Do you think it's worth $1500?"

"Probably, as it's a rare, beautiful stone but you may be able to get it a little cheaper. Some merchants like to bargain. You can try it."

We stopped at the General Store the next morning as we prepared to leave. More people than usual were there and we didn't know why until they gathered around to say goodbye.

This gesture was very emotional and I had to fight back the tears. I caught Mr. Adkins' eye and walked to his counter.

"I'll give you $1100 for the blue moonbeam."

He gave me a wry smile. "Nope, but I'll take $1400."

I'm not a person who likes to bargain but I gathered enough

courage to say, "How about $1200?"

"I can't take less than $1275. The stone comes with special papers and will be numbered and registered in the owner's name. If your fiancé keeps it, I'll fill out the paperwork and have it recorded."

"Sold," I said.

As Mr. Adkins wrapped it, I began to worry whether Tony would like it. Had I done a foolish thing? I would soon find out.

I tried not to look back as we left Sea Haven. I couldn't resist. The wind was strong and the waves were beating the shoreline in a rhythmic pattern. When the village was no longer in sight I sobbed uncontrollably.

Larry pulled over to the side of the road. I could tell from his body language he was not going to sympathize and baby me. His voice wasn't ugly but firm, "Lilly, do you know how fortunate you are? We found Cecil. We're going to have the illustrations we want and soon our documentary and your books will be going all over the world.

"Two men are in love with you and one is waiting for you now to come home and make wedding plans."

I knew he was right. I hit him on the arm and said, "Larry you're mean to me." We both laughed. Larry knew me all too well.

My problem is I get attached to people. I had been so sad when we left the doctors, nurses, and Achu and Lomin in that far away country on the other side of the world. Now I had made new friends and I hated to leave them. I guess it will always be that way.

Chapter 7

By the time we got off the plane I was in a great mood. Although it had only been a week I could hardly wait to see Tony, to feel his strong arms around me and to kiss him for the first time since he asked me to marry him. We spotted each other at the same time, and as he got close I could see his eyes—gorgeous eyes like I had never seen before. My mind went back to the first time I saw him, sitting on the corner of his desk looking at me with eyes that held me spellbound then and now.

"Lilly, I'm so glad you're home. I missed you like crazy."

"I'm glad to be home too and I can hardly wait for us to make wedding plans."

"I thought of nothing else while you were gone."

Teresa was there to meet Larry.

"Did you have a successful trip?" she asked.

"Yes, we did. We are very pleased with the illustrations and hope to have them in a month."

It was late by the time we got home. As we approached the gate with the words "Canaan" glowing in the dark, I spoke, "I'm back in the Promised Land."

I glanced at Tony. He smiled. Was that a tiny tear in the corner of his eye? I loved him all the more if that's possible.

He wanted to hear about Cecil and Sea Haven. He listened attentively as I described the interesting people and the quaint village. I didn't tell him about the blue moonbeam. That could wait until morning.

All I could think of now was Tony's love for me, his passion and his gentleness. Larry was right; I was very fortunate.

The smell of coffee woke me. No one made coffee as good as

Tony's, not even the finest restaurant. He came in with a coffee carafe and a small tray of strawberries and blueberries, my favorites. He dipped a large strawberry in heavy cream and fed me just like in the movies. Wow! There isn't a woman in the world who wouldn't enjoy this pampering.

Tony's hair was tousled, a few strands falling on his forehead; he hadn't shaved. The blue moonbeam earring would look good in his left ear now.

"Tony, I have a gift for you."

I went to the chest in the adjoining room and came back with the very small box.

"If you don't like it, please, please say so. I've made arrangements to take it back."

"I can't imagine what it is."

My heart was pounding as he opened it. I so much wanted him to like it.

"An earring, you want me to wear an earring?"

"It isn't just any earring. Read the brochure with it first."

It seemed like a long time before he said anything.

"It's beautiful. Where did you get it?"

"In Sea Haven at the General Store."

Then I told him about Mr. Adkins.

"I'll have to get my ear pierced."

"I know, but do you want to wear it?"

"Of course."

"You're not saying this just to please me?"

"No, I really like it. Do you want to go with me today to get my ear pieced?"

He smiled impishly, so characteristic of him.

"Yes," I said.

Tony decided he wanted his doctor to pierce his ear. He couldn't put the gem in for a few days. A gold post was inserted until there was no chance of infection.

"Lilly, would you like to get married in Hawaii?"

"What brought this on?"

"While you were gone I called Nell and Henry to tell them you had accepted my proposal. I was so excited I wanted to tell someone. Henry said I should call Bonnie, his sister in Hawaii. It had been a long time since we were in contact so I called.

"I told her the news and she said we ought to come to Hawaii and have an island ceremony. She told me about some of the customs, how beautiful and meaningful they are.

"'You could still have a traditional wedding but incorporate some of the special practices. I've been to several island weddings and they are unforgettable.'"

"It sounds exciting and different, Tony. How do you feel about it?"

"Bonnie is going to send some literature on Hawaiian weddings and we can decide then. We could spend our honeymoon there and stay as long as you would want to. But it doesn't matter, Lilly, where we get married."

I needed to call Mr. Adkins. One of the few telephones in Sea Haven was located at the General Store. Cecil did not have a phone. He said he didn't need it as he could always use the one downstairs. Mr. Adkins gave me the number before we left.

"General Store, Adkins speaking."

"Hello, Mr. Adkins, it's Lilly. I'm calling to tell you my check can be deposited. Tony likes the blue moonbeam very much and he had his ear pierced yesterday."

"Good, I'll have the registration papers ready when you come back."

"Cecil will call me when the paintings are ready and Larry and I will return to Sea Haven shortly thereafter."

Alexander and Josie were anxious to hear about my trip. They asked us to go with them to a new restaurant up the coast from Santa Barbara. When I finished my story, Tony said, "Lilly and I are thinking about going to Hawaii to be married."

Josie responded, "Sounds wonderful, how did you come up with that idea?"

Tony told them about his phone call to Bonnie.

"If you decide to do this, Josie and I would like to be guests. Lately we have discussed how much we would enjoy a trip to Hawaii."

The brochures from Bonnie came the following week and were very enticing. The more we read the more we were convinced this was what we wanted. Now we had to set a date. The booklet suggested the need to come to Hawaii at least two weeks prior to the wedding date.

Bonnie lived on Maui. The customs for weddings and other festivals differed from island to island.

Larry and I were going back to Sea Haven in three weeks so we decided to set the date six weeks ahead.

Cecil called a few days earlier than expected, but when I reached Larry by beeper he said he had to go to Washington to a meeting of the board for "Protect the Earth." He suggested that Tony go with me if possible.

I wanted Tony to meet the wonderful people of Sea Haven and see the village that seemed to be living in the past, at a slower, calmer pace.

Tony and I took the same early morning flight that Larry and I had taken only a month before. In many ways it seemed longer than a month but time has a way of playing tricks on us.

We rented a car in Seattle and were soon on our way to Sea Haven. It was different this time. I knew what to expect. In my imagination I could see the boy, Joshua, who led us up the stairs to Cecil's place; the friendly manner of Miriam and Cecil, and their warm hospitality; and Ezra's place and the Fish and Chips Diner. And then there was old Maudie and her legend of the water baby.

I related the story to Tony on our flight.

"What do you make of it, Tony?"

"I've never heard anything like it but that doesn't mean it's not true. Surely there are clues somewhere that could shed some light."

A few houses were in sight now, and when the water came in view I experienced the same peculiar feeling as before. This time I knew I had been there before but a sense of serenity impossible to describe was overtaking me.

Cecil was looking for us and was sitting on a bench in front of the General Store.

"I thought it was about time you got here, and this is Tony."

"Yes," I said. Cecil hugged me and said Miriam was preparing dinner for us.

He looked at Tony again. "Ah, I see you're wearing the blue moonbeam in your ear. It's very becoming."

"Thank you. I like it."

I loved it. Tony looked debonair and very romantic. I was anxious to show him off to the villagers.

That special aroma of Miriam's food was evident as we climbed the stairs. She opened the door. "And this is your fiancé. Welcome, come in."

Everything was exactly as before. I felt at home and a closeness, a special bond, with these people. This village held me in a magic spell.

Miriam noticed Tony's earring.

"It's perfect for you, Tony. Everyone in the village will want to meet you."

"Lilly, I know you're anxious to see the illustrations," Cecil said.

"Yes, I am."

"Come up to the studio." Cecil motioned for Tony to come too.

"It's just as Lilly described it; in fact, all that I've seen of Sea Haven is just as she told me."

I could hardly wait to see the pictures. I knew they would be perfect but as Cecil handed them to me one by one I was overcome, speechless, tears streaming down my face.

Cecil smiled. "Tony, I believe she likes them."

"I think that's an understatement. I'm amazed too. They're exactly what she and Larry have been looking for."

When I was able to speak, I said, "Now, we must talk about the price. This is a business deal and I don't want you to shortchange yourself."

"What about $100 for each illustration? I have done twelve if you want them all."

"Of course, I want all twelve. Please let me pay you $125 each; I insist."

"If that will make you happy, Lilly, I'll take it."

"I also must pay you for the paintings that were at the gallery. Larry has two, I have two and Tony has one."

Tony spoke up, "I have mine in my office and everyone who comes in comments on it and wants to know the artist. Now I can tell them I've met you."

"Thank you, Tony. It gives me great pleasure to know that my work is appreciated."

"I have a check with me, signed by Larry, and he told me to fill it out for whatever amount you want."

"What figure did you have in mind?" Cecil thoughtfully asked.

"The three of us put our heads together and this is our offer, $1000 for each painting plus $1500 commission for Jack, which he approved."

"I can't accept that much," Cecil said. "It's more than I've ever received for a painting."

"Well, you're not getting enough," I said. "Your work is very valuable."

He finally agreed and took the check for $5000.

It was getting late. "Tony, we must go. Ezra may lock you out if we stay too late."

"And Maudie?"

"She will wait up for me."

"How long can you stay?" Cecil asked as we were leaving.

"Three days. I want Tony to meet several people and enjoy the scenery."

"We'll expect you for dinner then tomorrow night."

Maudie was waiting on the porch.

"Tony, come and have breakfast with us in the morning. I cook better than Ezra."

"I'll look forward to it, Maudie."

I was awakened the next morning by what I thought was a voice saying, "Come with me." I saw no one. Maudie was still asleep. I looked towards the waterfront. The surf was up and large waves were coming ashore in rapid succession.

Barefoot and in my gown I walked slowly and methodically to the edge of the shoreline. I stood listening to the music of the waves mesmerized by the beauty and force of the waves.

I don't know how long I stood there but apparently quite a while. I suddenly felt Tony's arms around me.

"What are you doing here barefoot and in your gown? You're chilled and Maudie has been calling you."

I came back to reality and I said, "I'm sorry, I don't know."

"Come, get dressed, breakfast is ready."

Nothing else was said but I knew that Tony and Maudie were puzzled and concerned.

"Do you think the General Store is open now, Maudie?"

"Yes, they open early for the fishermen to get their supplies for the day."

Mr. Adkins was talking with a group of men when we entered.

"Ah, Lilly, it's you and your handsome fiancé. It's Tony, isn't it?"

"Yes, and you must be Mr. Adkins."

"Just call me Ad. I have your papers and registration ready. You are now a certified owner of a very rare blue moonbeam gem. It is very becoming, Tony, you'll have to fight off the ladies."

A man walked up and introduced himself as Luke and a young man with him as his son, Nathanael. "When you were here before I believe you and your friend wanted to go out on a schooner."

"That's right but we were told women were not allowed on schooners. Bad luck, I believe, was the reason."

"Yes, it's an old wives' tale and most people abide by it. Nathanael and I are not fishing today, so if you and your friend want to go out we'll take you."

"You're not afraid of bad luck?"

Luke laughed. "If we were working, that is, fishing, we wouldn't take you; but we are resting today. Meet us at the dock in an hour and we will show you the mechanics of a schooner. By the way, you probably should pack a lunch and drinks, also wear a wind breaker."

"Have you ever been on a schooner, Tony?" I asked.

"No, I haven't. I'm beginning to understand why you like Sea Haven."

When we reached the dock Luke and Nathanael were hoisting the sails. It was a thrilling, beautiful sight. I squeezed Tony's hand. He was excited too like a little boy ready to examine a new toy.

It was hard work getting a big schooner out of the dock and into the open waterway. Luke asked Tony to help. It was interesting to watch the three men cooperating in this joint endeavor.

When we reached open water it was easier to maneuver. Luke began to explain the mechanics and all the workings of a schooner.

I wanted to know more about Nathanael so I engaged him in conversation. "Tell me about yourself, Nathanael."

He was very handsome, yet had the rugged appearance of an outdoorsman. The effects of the sea were evident in his complexion—his blonde hair was bleached by the sun, but his blue eyes indicated a young man filled with compassion and sensitivity.

"I'm nineteen," he said. "My mother home schooled me until I was old enough to drive, then I entered high school in Tacoma about 15 miles away. I graduated last year."

"Now, what?" I asked. "Do you have plans or ambitions of any kind?"

"Not really. Mom died at the beginning of my senior year and Dad needs me. We make our living fishing and I couldn't leave him now."

"Have you ever thought of correspondence courses?"

"Only briefly as I don't know what I would like to study."

"Let me tell you how I became interested in conservation." I started my story by telling him of my teaching at the university, how I met Larry, and about our trip to the rain forest, the making of our documentary "Protect the Earth," and my books on the subject.

Nathanael spoke up, "I knew you came to see Cecil regarding art work connected with conservation but I didn't know the whole story.

It is very interesting and important."

"If you're interested in a correspondence course I can send you some brochures on what is available pertaining to conservation. Because your living is dependent on a pure environment you might consider courses on water pollution. I'm sure you are aware that many rivers and streams are becoming polluted."

I saw the excitement in this young man's eyes and it was rewarding for me to again be able to alert someone to the dangers threatening our world. Luke and Tony talked non-stop and I could tell Tony was having a good time. Luke said it was time for lunch.

It was amazing how easy it was to talk with Luke and Nathanael. This was true of all the people in Sea Haven.

I felt an attachment from the very beginning that surprised me due to different backgrounds and customs. Yet after traveling to the other end of the world I had learned that within each of us, from the natives of the rain forest to the fishermen in a small village, there is a thread, a chain that binds us together.

All of us experience fear at times; we have hopes and desires that vary from culture to culture, but one thread runs through all of us—to love and be loved, and be accepted.

This had been a special day. I looked at Tony. I could tell he had the same feeling.

We headed for the harbor and as the pier came in sight we saw the young boy, Joshua, waving to us.

As we came within hollering distance, he said, "Cecil wants you to come to dinner now." He ran off before we had time to talk with him.

"Thank you for a very extraordinary day and the pleasure of meeting you."

Tony tried to pay them but they wouldn't accept it.

"Nathanael, I'll send you the brochures I mentioned."

"Send them to the General Store. It's our post office."

Chapter 8

I had almost forgotten. I wanted to get in touch with Laura and Billy.

"Do you know the woman, Laura, and her son, Billy? They keep a sailboat here. Larry and I went sailing with them when we were here."

"I know to whom you have reference," said Luke, "but I haven't seen them lately. Have you, Nathanael?"

"No, but ask Joshua. I have seen him with Billy. Joshua is our village informer and messenger boy."

We learned from Cecil that Joshua was considered mentally challenged, that is, a slow learner. Also, Billy had befriended him and had taught him to read to a limited degree.

On the way to Cecil's home we saw Joshua and asked about Billy and his mother.

"His mother has been sick and they haven't been sailing in awhile."

"Do you know where they live?" I asked.

"Sure, you want to go there?"

"Yes, tomorrow. Will you show us the way?"

"I'll take you there, tomorrow."

Everything in Sea Haven was in walking distance. There were very few cars, which made the place more charming.

Joshua met us at the General Store at the appointed time eager to lead the way.

I asked, "Do you know what's wrong with Laura?"

"No, she goes to the doctor a lot."

Billy saw us coming and ran to meet us.

"How is your mother today?" I inquired.

"Some better." He looked at Tony and said, "Where's Larry?"

"He had to go to Washington, D.C. on business. I'm Tony and I'm going to marry Lilly."

"Oh." Billy looked at me and said, "Did you bring the stuff you promised?"

I laughed. "Yes, I brought the stuff." I handed him a large manila envelope crammed full.

"Wow! Thanks."

"You have a lot to read now."

Laura came out on the porch to greet us. She looked pale and thin. I was very concerned.

"This is Tony," I said. "We're going to be married in Hawaii in a few weeks."

"Wonderful! Congratulations!"

"Laura," I said, "you don't look well. What's wrong?"

She ushered us into the living room. "Billy, show Tony your room and tell him about your project."

Joshua spoke up, "Tony, I know where the Pacific Ocean is. I found it on Billy's map."

"Great," said Tony.

Tony doesn't have much opportunity to be with young people and he told me he misses this association. It was also good for the boys to be with a man, as neither one had a father.

"The day after you and Larry left I went to the doctor in Seattle. I had been feeling extremely tired and no appetite either. Extensive testing showed a malignancy but at this point the doctors don't know how much it has spread and the source of its beginning."

I was in tears and said, "I'm so sorry, and I don't know what to say."

"I'm taking medication and feel some better and after we get the final results of testing, the decision will be made whether or not to have chemotherapy treatment."

"I hope that won't be necessary."

"I hope not too. Billy is behind on his school work as there have been days I didn't feel like teaching him, but he's very intelligent and can learn many things on his own."

"I want to see Billy's room," I said. About that time Billy called from upstairs.

"Come up, Lilly, and see my room."

On each side of one large window were two bookshelves from floor to the top of the windowsills filled with books. The other walls were covered with maps, large and small, showing all the bodies of water and earth. I was astonished and very impressed. It was more of a school room than a bedroom.

"Billy, this is wonderful," I said.

I could tell he was pleased.

Joshua was beaming too. It was evident he was proud of his friend and didn't appear the least bit jealous.

Tony was studying the maps carefully, "I've never seen anything like this, Billy. When will you finish high school?"

"Maybe three years, according to how fast I move through the required courses. Mom has to fill out papers every month."

"I want to keep up with your progress and if I can help you after you finish high school, please let me know." Tony handed Billy his business card. "You can call me anytime and in the meantime if you need advice I'll be glad to help."

It was time to say goodbye. "Laura," I said, "I want to keep informed of your health. Here is my phone number. You may call me or have someone else call."

"Thank you, this means a lot to Billy and me. You can call the General Store and Joshua will deliver a message from you."

Again I had to fight back the tears. I was easily touched by people and became involved in their lives almost without realizing it.

Tony and I left the next day in mid-afternoon for the drive to Seattle. We had to take the night flight. It was so hard leaving this time, as I didn't know when I would come back to Sea Haven, if ever.

Everyone had gathered at the General Store to see us off. One by one I looked into their eyes: Cecil, the artist, and Miriam, our hosts for delicious meals. No words would come. Dear sweet old Maudie wearing an apron, pulling out a handkerchief to wipe the tears; Ezra, Mr. Adkins, Luke and Nathanael. It was a time that would forever be pressed indelibly in my mind. Tony too felt the intensity of the moment as I leaned on him for support.

I was glad it was a night flight. We could sleep and not feel the need to talk. Both of us were drained from the emotions of the day. I settled down quickly with a big, fluffy pillow. Tony kissed me tenderly every now and then. What would I do without Tony's gentleness, compassion and love? Just before drifting into deep sleep I remembered Larry's words, "Lilly, you're a very fortunate woman."

Chapter 9

Larry was due back from Washington in two days. I was anxious for him to see the illustrations and get them to the publisher. Already we were receiving requests for the books. Many schools and universities wanted them for studies on the environment.

I had several things to think about. Now that I was marrying Tony I had to decide what to do with my apartment. It was so convenient to the university but I realized I should give up my work there. As I became more involved in "Protect the Earth" there wasn't enough time to do justice to the seminars and lectures on Family Relationships. It was a very important field but there were others who could carry on effectively.

Larry's meetings in Washington went well and he was encouraged that more and more groups were becoming aware of the need to protect our environment.

He wanted to hear about our trip to Sea Haven. He was very pleased with the illustrations, and inquired about Cecil, Miriam, and the others. I told him about Luke and Nathanael and our day with them on the schooner. He was very concerned about Laura and said, "There may come a time when we'll need to help Billy."

"I thought of that too," I said. "We must keep in touch with them. Billy promised to call me or Tony if he needs anything. I also gave him your number."

I was still tired from our trip. I think it was mostly emotional. I was sleeping late each day and being lazy. Some days Tony would go to his office and leave me to sleep. He knew I needed time to put Sea Haven in its proper place in my mind. Also we were leaving for Hawaii in ten days and our wedding was three weeks away.

I had decided to buy my wedding dress in Maui. This was Bonnie's suggestion; I wouldn't have to transport it and also I wanted an authentic island wedding dress.

I was day dreaming and dozing when I heard Josie rattling pots and pans in the kitchen. Surely I could find something constructive to do today. I turned to look at the clock and saw a note on the table. It read: "Lilly, meet me in the Empire Room of the Albany Hotel for dinner at 7:00. I have a very busy day and to save time I asked Alexander and Josie to drive you. Don't drive your car."

I was awake now and went to the kitchen to have coffee. Josie's coffee was good but not like Tony's.

"Josie, what's going on with Tony?"

"I don't know, Lilly. He asked if we would drive you to the Albany. All I know is he left carrying a garment bag so I guess he's going to change clothes."

"Josie, I don't have anything to wear."

My wardrobe consisted of business suits for teaching and casual clothing. My social life was almost non-existent until I met Tony.

"You'll have time to shop, Lilly. It's only eleven o'clock. I think you need something very special for this evening."

"I think so too, but I don't know where to go. Will you go with me?"

"There's a nice shop in that new area near the edge of town. Let's try it."

As soon as we entered I realized the shop was elegant and exclusive, and probably very expensive. Oh, well, I hadn't bought anything in a long time so I could afford to indulge myself.

We told the lovely young woman who approached us that I wanted a special dress for an evening out with my fiancé. She said her name was Judith, as she invited us to sit on a luxurious sofa while she brought dresses one by one to us. I always know immediately whether or not I like something—nothing so far.

Another woman came up to Judith and said something not audible to us.

Judith said, "A dress has just come in that you may like if you'll give us a few minutes to press it."

Josie and I looked at each other. "We don't have anything to lose except a little time," she said.

We were offered tea and cookies and Judith said, "Will you need anything else for this evening?"

"Possibly shoes, but I'll have to find a dress first."

Another customer entered the shop and we learned from her that we should have made an appointment, but we didn't know.

Almost the minute I saw it I knew it was the one—blue chiffon with small peach colored flowers making an uneven but pleasing design as if the flowers had been scattered on a field of blue. The dress was straight and to the floor, a short sleeve stopping above the elbow, a separate blue silk slip.

I looked at Josie; she nodded in approval. I could hardly wait to try it on. It fit perfectly and Judith said, "It has a blue silk long sleeve jacket that goes with it. Ah, here it is." A girl opened the door and handed it to Judith.

When I walked out to show Josie she gasped. "It's perfect; it's the most beautiful dress I have ever seen."

Judith smiled and said, "But that's not all. It has a peach colored slip and a short sleeve long vest to make another outfit. It will be ready for you to see in minutes."

I couldn't even begin to imagine the price.

"I have blue shoes and peach shoes to match."

As I was trying on the shoes she said, "I believe I have seen you before. You look very familiar."

"I'm sorry," I said. "I failed to introduce myself. I'm Lilly Tompkins. Maybe you have seen the documentary I'm in. It is being shown in schools, theaters and television."

"Yes, that's it. You and a man are in the rain forest and you have a cast on your foot. What happened?"

"I slipped on a loose rock and broke my foot while in the jungle. The man is Larry Mathis, close friend and business partner in an organization called 'Protect the Earth.'"

We almost forgot about the shoes. I decided the peach ones were best and maybe would go with more things.

"The peach slip and vest are ready to try now," Judith said. They made a completely different look and I liked it too.

"I'm afraid to ask the price," I said.

Judith smiled, "It's $1200, but you have two ensembles. The shoes are $75, very reasonable."

"Yes. I'm getting married in Hawaii in three weeks and the dress will be great for some of the parties there."

"This dress was made for Lilly, don't you agree?" Judith said, turning to Josie.

"No doubt about it. I have never seen you look more beautiful. I have a small silk peach evening bag I'm going to give you as a wedding gift."

I was so excited I could hardly stand it. "Josie, do you think I paid too much for the dress? I'm never this extravagant."

"No, because you have two different outfits. Don't give it a thought, consider it part of your wedding wardrobe."

As I entered the lobby of the Albany Hotel I felt that everyone was looking at me which wasn't true at all; nevertheless I was self-conscious and a little uneasy, although I was pleased with my appearance.

I guess I had spent too many years in the plain clothes required by the university; also I had been very comfortable in the shirts and pants I wore in the jungle, and after that the ordinary clothes suitable for Sea Haven.

I approached the desk and gave my name.

"Yes, Mrs. Tompkins. Mr. Saunders is waiting in the Empire Room. I'll take you up. It's on the 12th floor."

Tony was standing near the elevator and when the door opened and I stepped out he took one look and said "Wow! Lilly, wow."

"Josie and I went shopping."

"You did indeed."

"Josie says I should wear it for our wedding. What do you think?"

"I think it's lovely and would be fine unless you find something in Maui you like better. One thing for sure I have never seen you look more beautiful."

"I've ordered our wine," said Tony just as the waiter appeared. I noticed the label immediately, "Promised Land."

"Oh, Tony, it's your wine."

"No, it's our wine from our vineyard."

"I have something for you, Lilly."

He reached in his jacket pocket and pulled out a small box. When someone gives me an unexpected gift I'm like a child, anxious to find out what it is. I didn't think it was a ring; I told Tony when we first met that the only jewelry I liked was earrings and necklaces. I was totally unprepared as I opened the lid.

"Don't scream, Lilly," Tony said with that mischievous grin that slowly creeps across his face from time to time.

Earrings, but not just any earrings. They looked like blue moonbeam stones.

"It can't be," I said.

"Oh, but it is."

"When and how?" I asked.

"One day when we were in the General Store Mr. Adkins took me aside and said that something had just come in I might be interested in. I told him I would have to come back later. I went back the next morning while you were at Maudie's."

"I still can't believe it," I said.

The earrings were tear drops about 1 3/4 inches long. A small stone earring about the size of Tony's was at the top and a larger one was dangling from the top one joined by a small silver stem.

"Put them on," Tony said. I was so excited I couldn't hold them so Tony put them in. I already had pierced ears.

"They were made for you, Lilly. I think Mr. Adkins knew that. They had only been in the store two days when he told me about them."

"Let's dance, Lilly." The song was "Love is a Many Splendored Thing." His lips touched my hair and my face. At that moment I knew I was the happiest woman in the world.

Henry and Nell planned to go to Hawaii for our wedding, and also his cousin, Bobby, whom I had met at the square dance. They would arrive one week before the wedding.

Alexander and Josie would be traveling with Tony and me and we were leaving in two days. Nell, Henry, Bobby and Tony were going to stay at a nearby hotel. One of the customs was that the bride and groom could not reside under the same roof for at least three weeks prior to the wedding.

During the flight Tony told me about Bonnie.

"I never knew her as well as I did Henry. When she was eighteen she went to San Diego. At the university there she met Marco, a young man from the islands, and they married a year later. When they finished their education they moved to Maui."

I had never been to Hawaii so I was excited about many things. Tony had visited several times and Alexander and Josie had been a number of years ago.

We invited Larry and Teresa to the wedding but they declined. He had another appointment in Washington. I had mixed feelings but it was just as well that they couldn't come. Although Larry was the one who introduced me to Tony it would have been a little difficult for everyone. We were able to set aside our true feelings, place them in their proper perspective, yet remain good friends and business partners.

Bonnie met us at the airport. She rushed up to Tony and grabbed him.

"Tony, you are more handsome than ever." Then she noticed his earring. "I can't believe it, I thought you were too conservative to wear jewelry."

I spoke up and said, "I guess I'm responsible for the earring. There's a story connected with it. We'll tell you later."

"Oh, Lilly, I'm so glad to meet you. I've wondered what you were like and how you would look."

I must have blushed. Tony said, "Lilly, Bonnie has always been open and candid."

"It's an admirable characteristic," I said.

Tony introduced Alexander and Josie. Then Bonnie said, "Come, the car is close by. We'll get you registered at your hotel."

The next day we discussed wedding plans with Bonnie. She said, "Your wedding can be in the church, or on the beach, or in my garden facing the channel."

This was an easy decision for me; however, I would have been happy with either one of the locations. I knew Tony and Bonnie were waiting for me to speak up.

"I would like for it to be in your garden under an arbor facing the beach so we can see and hear the waves."

"One of the most beautiful Hawaiian weddings I have seen," said Bonnie, "was a circle formed by young people ages thirteen to not over nineteen that surrounded the couple during the ceremony. Many young people are desirous of being a part of the circle and they put their names on the church register. Then they are chosen on the basis of character and moral values."

"I like that idea very much," I said, and Tony said it sounded nice to him.

"What do these young people wear and are there boys and girls?"

"Yes, the boys wear the same attire as the groom; the girls wear white chiffon dresses with a different color slip under each one, usually blue, peach, green or mauve."

"And the groom?"

"He wears white satin pants, white silk shirt, long sleeved, and a white satin vest."

Bonnie continued, "Brides have more choices. Most brides wear white or a combination of white with pastel colors; however, I have seen one or two when the bride wore a very bright color combined with white. The most unusual wedding I have ever seen was the one in which the bride's dress was made of live flowers—white orchids and camellias. It was beautiful!"

"Lilly," Bonnie asked, "would you and Josie like to go shopping today?"

"Yes, but first Tony and I want to tell you about our earrings."

I told them about Sea Haven and how I found the blue moonbeam stone in an earring and bought it for Tony.

Then Tony told about our trip together when he found my earrings.

I spoke up, "I want to wear the earrings at my wedding and would like to find a dress that would compliment them."

"That may not be easy," Bonnie said.

We made the rounds of all the shops Bonnie thought would have something. Even though all the dresses were beautiful, nothing caught my eye as being the one. I knew I would know immediately.

Bonnie said, "Let's stop now for lunch and I'll think about some other place to look."

After lunch we drove about fifty miles down the coast to a shop Bonnie had heard about.

We looked at several dresses and were about to give up when Jan, the sales lady, said, "Wait, we had a shipment that just came in. Let me look."

I had heard that before when I bought the dress for the dinner with Tony. Jan came back in a few minutes with *the* dress. I could hardly believe it.

"That's it," said Josie.

It was soft, flowing, thin material white and blue, not actually a design; but as I looked at it, I could see white, billowy clouds floating in a pale blue sky over darker blue water. A perfect match for the earrings. The others didn't see this until I pointed it out. It fit perfectly. I liked the style—plain, straight, good neckline, suitable for a necklace, and sleeveless. A large scarf or shawl of the same material came with it. I had my wedding dress! I decided to wear white silk ballet type slippers. The shop had exactly what I wanted. I was ready to relax.

Chapter 10

The days went by quickly. Henry, Nell and Bobby arrived and we had a celebration. One nice thing about weddings, they bring family members together who haven't seen one another for a long time. However, funerals do the same thing.

Tony and I decided to write our own vows. Bonnie had arranged for some of her friends to play Hawaiian music and a couple was going to sing love songs. The reception would be on Bonnie's lawn, patio and terrace. Everything was in place.

For a fleeting moment I wondered where Larry and Teresa were. Was Larry sorry he didn't come? No, probably not.

I woke early the day of my wedding. The beach could be seen from our hotel but it was too far to walk. I called to Josie in the adjoining room. "Josie, are you awake?"

"Yes, Lilly, are you all right?"

"I'm fine, I want to walk on the beach a while."

"I'll go with you. We'll get a hotel car."

"If you don't mind, I want to go alone. I'll be fine. The hotel driver can take me and come back in an hour."

"If you're sure."

"I'm sure, don't worry."

I felt so at home on the beach near water. The waves were peaceful and calm, coming in slowly and methodically. My mind drifted back to Sea Haven—dear Cecil and Miriam. I wondered what Cecil was painting. I could visualize them in their studio above the General Store. Was Joshua running errands for someone?

Old Maudie was probably sweeping the porch; Luke and Nathanael may be hoisting the sails on the schooner; Laura and Billy could be doing homework; Mr. Adkins was selling fishing supplies and the rowdy bunch at the Fish and Chips Diner were drinking beer and telling tall tales.

Tears were running down my face. Sea Haven and the people there held a special place in my heart. The hotel driver was blowing the horn. I had a wedding to go to—my own.

Bonnie was responsive to most of the plans for our wedding and no one ever had a more beautiful one. Everything was perfect.

When Tony and I met under the arbor and the circle of young people closed, I looked at him in the white satin suit that complimented his dark eyes and hair; and for a moment I wished that time could stand still. His earring made him even more distinguished, and I felt that my dress and earrings were beyond comparison.

We had made plans to spend a week at a honeymoon getaway on another part of the island, and after the reception a large canoe resembling a kayak took us there. It was very romantic to ride away on the water and wave to the people on shore.

Alexander and Josie planned to leave in a few days to return to Canaan and Promised Land. They left three nephews in charge but were anxious to get back.

Henry, Nell and Bobby were going to stay on a few weeks so we would visit with them after our trip.

Our villa was in a remote setting of unbelievable beauty. Tropical plants and flowers were everywhere. We had a private drive and beach and were completely secluded until we were driven the two miles to the restaurant. If we wanted food brought in that could be arranged also.

Several mornings I slipped out early to walk on the beach. I was sure the waves were calling me. I'm sure Tony didn't understand but he was patient and tolerant, never questioning.

There were days when I felt that Tony and I were the only two people in the world.

It was time to go back to Bonnie's house. We didn't know how long Henry, Nell and Bobby would be there and it was almost time for all of us to go back to the mainland.

In the weeks and months that followed we were busy. Tony had some contracts for directing various projects; I decided to limit my work at the university to two seminars a year as I became more involved in "Protect the Earth." Our documentary and books were so widely publicized we were even recognized on the streets.

I went with Larry on several public appearances and lectures but I preferred to stay at Canaan and enjoy my life with Tony.

One day Tony received a call from Nathanael in Sea Haven. His father had died recently and talking with Tony he said, "Even though Sea Haven has always been my home, I have the desire now to go to college. I remember the conversation with you and Lilly and I want to study conservation and the environment."

Tony told him of a university near Santa Barbara and that he would help him get in.

Nathanael said, "I don't have much money, but I can sell the fishing equipment and the schooner plus our small house and have something to start on."

Tony told him not to worry about the money. Perhaps a scholarship was available and if not, we would help him.

Nathanael had good news. Cecil and Miriam were married and Miriam was pregnant. Joshua was still the village messenger. Laura was taking chemotherapy treatments and was improving. Billy was going to school nearby.

I was always nostalgic when I heard news from Sea Haven. It had a feeling of peace and calm not found any other place in the world.

Josie was calling me, "Lilly, telephone call for you."

"Who is it?"

"I don't know but she sounds like an old woman."

"Who could it be?"

"Hello, this is Lilly."

"Lilly, this is Mable, your cousin, in Charleston."

"Mable, how are you? I haven't heard from you in years. How did you find me?"

"Through your colleague, Larry Mathis. His number is on a

brochure regarding 'Protect the Earth.'"

I was very surprised to hear from Mable. She was a distant cousin and our families were not very close. I could not imagine what prompted her to call.

Mable continued, "Your family's old home place has sold again and the new owners found an old trunk in the basement. Your mother's name is on it. They didn't feel free to open it and I don't want to either. I think you should come and go through the contents."

I thought to myself, "What do I want with an old trunk filled with old stuff?"

Mable was still talking, "You know sometimes old trunks contain valuable information about families not found elsewhere. I really think you should come."

I know very little about my parents, so I was thinking maybe I should go. I might find interesting information from the past.

"Mable, I'll talk it over with Tony and call you back."

"Good, I would like to see you."

I told Tony about the call and he said, "Sure, we'll make the trip. It sounds like an adventure."

Four days later we flew to Charleston. It is a beautiful city—trees dripping with Spanish moss, old trees with gnarled branches and trunks, the smell of magnolias and lilacs, large houses with white columns indicative of days gone by, another era.

Mable was waiting for us and it was nice to see a relative again, even a distant one. She was charming and hospitable as a Southern woman should be. She insisted that we have coffee, or tea with Southern tea cakes before we talked of anything else.

"Tony," she said finally, "how did you meet Lilly? It's fascinating to learn how people meet and fall in love."

Tony was very anxious to tell our story and I sat back in admiration as he began with my interest in conservation, our connection on "Protect the Earth" and the pursuit of a mysterious artist.

Then I told her about Canaan, Promised Land, the beauty of the vineyards, and about our friends Alexander and Josie. I described our beautiful wedding as she appeared spellbound like a young girl listening to a fairy story.

I was beginning to be more and more curious about the trunk but I didn't want to appear rude when she was enjoying our conversation.

At last Mable said, "Come to the garage. I had the trunk brought up from the basement. It was covered in dust and the initials were barely visible." She had chairs for us and said, "I'll leave the two of you alone to open it. I need to tend to our supper."

As I lifted the top my heart was pounding. Why was I so nervous? It's just an old trunk, probably nothing of interest to me.

A musty smell escaped as I picked up clothes, small boxes, pictures and odds and ends. I had the feeling I was invading the life of someone, my mother, the person I don't remember.

On top was a long envelope and the words "To my daughter Lilly." I asked Tony to sit close and read the letter to me.

> Dear Lilly, my precious little girl,
>
> I don't know if you'll ever see and read this letter. I'm sorry I kept this secret for so long, but it was more painful than I could bear.
>
> When I was in high school our Senior Class went on a trip to Washington, D.C. Several other high schools' classes were there also. While going through one of the buildings I caught the eye of a boy who was staring at me.
>
> He walked closer and said, "Hi gorgeous, I'm going to marry you." I'm sure my cheeks turned crimson, but I managed to say, "Sure, yeah, sure."
>
> "You just wait and see. My name's Jacob, what's yours?"
>
> "Mary," I answered.
>
> "I'll find you tomorrow," he said as his group moved on.
>
> My group was moving in a different direction and I thought, well I'll never see him again. He's trying to be

cute and impress his friends.

The next day in a cafeteria line for lunch HE walked up, "Hi, Mary,"

"Hi Jacob."

I was very surprised. He was tall, good-looking, muscular, with an impish grin, dark blue eyes and dark hair.

"May I get in line with you and have lunch at your table?"

"I guess so," I stammered, completely off guard.

"You're from Charleston, South Carolina, aren't you?"

"Yes," I said, "how did you know?"

"I asked our principal to find out," he said.

"And where are you from, Jacob?"

"Seattle, Washington."

"You're a long way from home."

"Yes."

We talked about our schools and things we were interested in.

We went our separate ways after lunch. He called to me as he hurried to join his group, "I'll see you tomorrow, I'll find you."

The next day we met with three other high schools at Georgetown University to listen to a motivational speaker and afterwards for a fellowship hour on the campus lawn.

Jacob rushed up. "Let's talk," he said. He grabbed my hand and we walked to a nearby bench under a big tree. I'll never forget that day, Lilly, I think I fell in love at that minute.

Jacob was talking, "We're leaving tomorrow. Here's my address and phone number. May I have yours?"

"Yes."

"I have to see you again," he said.

"There's a great distance between us, but we can talk

from time to time."

"May I kiss you good bye?"

I didn't answer but he knew, as I did not pull away when he got closer.

To this day, Lilly, I can feel his tender kiss—the ecstasy of first love.

At this point Tony stopped me and said, "Lilly, you're tired. Mable has supper ready. Can we finish reading tomorrow when we're rested?"

Even though I was anxious and fascinated I agreed. I slept very well and after Mable's delicious breakfast of country ham, scrambled eggs, homemade biscuits, and gravy we were ready for a walk.

Chapter 11

Charleston is beautiful any time of the year but especially in spring—azaleas are everywhere and some camellias are still in bloom. Lilacs in full bloom were hanging from trellises, arbors and fences.

"Lilly, how could you leave such a beautiful place?" Tony asked.

"I don't really know except I felt my life was stagnant and I needed to move in a different direction."

I wanted to get back to the letter. It was strange reading a letter written to me from my mother whom I never knew very well. I remember she was beautiful and kind but she seemed sad most of the time. She had a faraway look in her eyes and appeared to be wrapped in mystery.

My mother never mentioned my father and I didn't feel comfortable asking about him. Shortly before my grandmother died I asked her but she didn't know.

Maybe now I could learn more. I knew also that Mable was probably very curious so I said, "Mable, when I finish reading the letter, you may read it. I think you have the right."

The letter continued,

> After our class returned and we settled into our school routine I still couldn't get Jacob off my mind. Should I call first or wait for him? I decided to write a short letter telling him I enjoyed meeting him. He called immediately.
>
> For the next five months we wrote to each other and called when our parents permitted, which wasn't often as phone calls were expensive.
>
> Jacob enrolled in a community college in Seattle and

I persuaded my parents to let me work at a florist and study flower design temporarily. I knew Jacob and I were in love but my parents weren't convinced.

One night Jacob called and he sounded distraught. "I have to see you; I want to be with you," he said continuing, "my parents have an idea. They wonder if your parents would allow you to come here and go to Community College."

"I doubt it," I told him. "With your approval," Jacob said, "my parents will write your parents." For several weeks they corresponded and talked by phone. Finally they agreed to let me enter the college there on a trial basis.

Three months passed and our love was so powerful and overwhelming that we decided to get married. My mother and father flew to Seattle and in a small chapel in the country away from the sights and sounds of the city we were married.

"I told you, Mary, I was going to marry you." I smiled as he held me in his arms. "Yes, you did."

We only had four free days from school but Jacob said he knew of a fishing village south of Seattle that sounded quiet and peaceful.

We got to the village at sunset just as the sun was sinking into the horizon where the ocean meets the sky. Their sailboats had lowered their sails and headed for the harbor and schooners in the distance were coming in with their catch of fish.

We were spellbound and I said, "Oh Jacob, I would like to live here."

At this point I dropped the letter; I was trembling, blood was rushing to my head and I was about to black out. Tony called to Mabel, "Mabel, do you have ammonia or smelling salts, come quick." I passed out and the next thing I remember was Tony and Mabel leaning over me as I inhaled ammonia.. They quickly removed it when I started coughing. "I think we should put the letter away for awhile," Tony said. "This is too much for you."

I was holding onto Tony, still trembling slightly. "NO," I said, "I have to go on now."

"Let's have a glass of lemonade first," Mabel said.

My mind drifted back in time to my childhood—those carefree days when life was simple and uncomplicated—those days when I sat on the veranda sipping a tall glass of lemonade. My entire world was centered in Charleston. As far as I was concerned there was no other place.

Now things were different. I pictured Larry and me in the rain forest, the documentary, the books, the paintings, falling in love with Tony, finding Cecil, my wedding in Hawaii. It was almost too much—the similarity of two fishing villages or was it one and the same?

I wasn't sure I wanted to know and yet it was imperative that I find out. Revived by the lemonade I slowly picked up the page of the letter where we stopped.

My mother's writing changed as if she held the pen nervously,

> Jacob and I sat on the beach in silence watching the waves come ashore in quiet, rhythmic motions almost whispering as they rolled in. No one was in sight. The sleepy little village was shrouded in darkness, and Jacob and I made love in the water. The ecstasy of the moment transcended time or space and we were lost in our love blended with earth, sky and water.

I began to cry. I was reading my mother's words as she described her most intimate moments and I felt like an intruder. Tony said, "I hate to see you so upset. Are you sure you're up to this?"

"I must go on, it's my mother's story and mine."

We continued reading:

> When the four days had passed we were more

convinced than ever that we wanted to live in this village, but how? We were attending college in Seattle and our parents would be very disappointed if we dropped out. The idea occurred to me that perhaps we could take correspondence courses.

This plan worked out and we moved to the village we had fallen in love with. The name of the village was Sea Haven.

I dropped the letter. "Oh Tony, I'm not believing this. It's impossible and yet it's here on the written page." Tony was so stunned he was speechless.

Mabel brought a plate of sandwiches and a bowl of fresh fruit and although I wasn't sure I could eat due to the state of my mind, I felt I needed nourishment to go on. There were two pages left.

Jacob got a job with two fishermen and studied at night. I studied during the day and walked on the beach. It was so peaceful, so beautiful, so calm. I watched in awe as the fishermen hoisted their sails each morning as the waves came ashore in their never-ending pattern.

I soon discovered I was pregnant and we were very happy even though we were young and not financially secure. The time passed quickly and we discussed names. Jacob said, "A girl should be called 'Lilly' for water lily," and I said, "a boy should be named 'Moses' because he was drawn out of the water." We were certain the baby was conceived in the water.

In my 7th month it was necessary for Jacob to take the fishing boat out alone. His partners were unable to go and several customers were depending on a large catch. Jacob said he would be gone at least two days. I waded out into ankle deep water and watched as he pulled away from the shore. He waved and called out, "Love you, Mary." I fought back the tears and waved.

We hadn't been apart since our marriage.

The time passed fairly quickly as I was making some clothes for the baby and the time was getting closer. Jacob didn't come home the second day. On the third day I couldn't keep my mind on the sewing. Instead I spent most of the day at the pier looking into the distance expecting to see the boat come into view at any minute.

Several days went by and the village people were concerned so they formed search groups to go out. After three weeks the search was called off. Nothing could be found.

I was devastated but I tried to keep up my strength for the baby. Every morning at dawn I went to the water's edge gazing into the horizon still hoping. Two months later as I walked to the beach I felt sharp pains and I knew the time had come. No one was in sight and I sat in the water not knowing what to do. A fine mist brushed my face with a refreshing spray and the gentle waves came in covering me to the waist. As the waves went back out into the ocean the baby practically dropped into my hands.

What was I to do? Completely alone except for this new life I knew I couldn't give up. A young woman looking for seashells found me and sent someone for the village doctor.

The baby was you, my precious Lilly. I called you my "Water Lilly" because you were born in the water. You were beautiful and good but I was so lonely without Jacob, the love of my life.

When you were three months old I decided to go home. The memories at Sea Haven were too painful and I couldn't bear to say goodbye to anyone. I was able to ride to Seattle with a salesman passing through. The man was nice and took us to the airport in Seattle.

All these years I kept the secret and now I feel I have

done you and my family a great injustice. Please forgive me. If you find this letter I hope you will visit Sea Haven and remember the love your father and I shared. I wish I could live to see you a grown woman but my time is short. Oh, my Lilly, my water baby—I love you so much.

Your mother,
Mary Anna

I was sobbing uncontrollably and Tony was holding me and comforting me. Mabel was crying too and we were silent for a long time. Then a thought came to me. Now I know why I'm drawn to water and to the waves of the ocean. I understand why I sensed I had been to Sea Haven before. I had been there. I was born of the water and the waves, as sailboats in the distance and schooners in the harbor made ready for their sails to be raised in the early morning light.

I relaxed and a calm came over me. "Tony, can you believe it? I'm the water baby."

"Yes, Lilly, this letter explains many things. Now you know who you are and why you are this way. I think it's wonderful, Lilly, I love you."

"I love you, too, Tony."

We decided to stay a few days and talk more with Mabel. Also we needed to make arrangements to have the trunk sent to our home in Santa Barbara.

In the days that followed there were times when I had the feeling the letter was all a dream. It took a while for reality to sink in.

I was anxious to tell Larry, "I have something amazing to tell you. Is Teresa in town?"

"Yes."

"Can you meet us at the Coral Restaurant this evening?"

Tony made copies of the letter and as soon as our wine was served I handed Larry and Teresa a copy.

While they were reading Tony and I danced. The band was playing one of our favorites, "There Will Never Be Another You."

Larry and Teresa were so stunned no one spoke for a minute then

Larry said, "They say sometimes truth is stranger than fiction. This is almost unbelievable."

"This explains many things, doesn't it?" I said.

"Indeed it does," Larry replied. "What do you plan to do now?"

"Tony and I plan to go to Sea Haven as soon as possible. Can you and Teresa go too?"

Teresa had never been to Sea Haven.

"I would like to go," Teresa said.

I called Mr. Adkins at the General Store and asked him to tell Cecil to call me. "Cecil and Miriam have a phone now; here's the number," Mr. Adkins said.

Cecil was glad and surprised to hear from me.

"Cecil, I have an amazing story to tell you and we're coming to Sea Haven." I explained that Larry and his wife were coming too.

"I'll make arrangements for you. We now have a small lodge that is very nice. When will you be here?"

"Thursday."

"Miriam says she is anxious for you to see our son, Joseph; he's crawling and trying to stand."

This trip to Sea Haven would be different. Many things had changed. I had changed. As we approached the ridge overlooking Sea Haven and the water, the same strange feeling I had experienced so many times came over me again. This time I knew—I had been there before.

"Stop the car, Larry, I need to get out a minute." In the distance I once again saw the sailboats gliding silently on the calm water. Some boats were in the harbor waiting patiently for someone to take them out so they could display their sails like butterflies riding on a morning breeze.

This was the place of my birth. I was a part of the earth, sky and water here. I forgot everything except the completeness—the loose ends were tied—I had come full circle.

"This must be a wonderful feeling, Lilly." I did not hear Tony as he walked quietly to where I stood.

"Yes, it's indescribable."

The new lodge in Sea Haven was a welcome addition to the village and was built to compliment the quaint scenic beauty of the place. Made of logs it was rustic in character and looked as if it had been there for years.

I looked out the window of our second story room facing the harbor. "Tony, look!"

The sailboats were coming in and the schooners in the distance were headed for the shore. The waves in their never-ending movements were creeping upon the beach.

I was trembling and Tony held me. He, too, felt the emotion of the moment.

"This is your world, Lilly, your heritage. I can feel your vitality and your excitement."

Larry and Teresa knocked on our door.

"Oh, Lilly," Teresa said, "I know why you love this place. It is so peaceful and tranquil. We may be looking at the actual place where you were born in the water. I have goose bumps thinking about it."

"I do too," I said.

Larry smiled. "When we came here looking for an artist in this remote area, Lilly, I never dreamed we would uncover this incredible story."

"No, Larry, I didn't either, but now, I understand my strange feelings. I was beginning to think I had lost my mind."

Cecil and Miriam were expecting us for dinner. "It's time to go," said Tony. "We don't want to be late."

I could hardly wait to show my letter to Cecil.

The lodge was close enough to the General Store that we could walk comfortably. Cecil must have seen us from his window. He was at the bottom of the steps waiting for us. He spoke first. "It's wonderful the four of you are here together. Miriam and I have looked forward to your visit and also to meeting your wife, Larry."

"I'm so happy to finally be here," Teresa said. "I've heard so much about Sea Haven and nothing I was told is exaggerated. I'm already in love with it."

Miriam was at the head of the stairs holding Joseph. "We are happy to see you," she said. "Come in." Everything looked the same except for a few toys scattered around and the high chair in the corner. As usual the aroma from the kitchen was tantalizing.

Joseph was a beautiful baby. He smiled at each one of us and won our hearts completely. He held out his arms for Teresa to pick him up and of course this pleased her.

Cecil said, "We are curious about what you have to tell us."

"Let's wait until after dinner," I said. "I have a long letter I want you to read."

Having the baby had not interfered with Miriam's cooking ability. She always prepared something different and this evening was no exception.

Teresa and Larry played with Joseph so Cecil and Miriam could read the letter together. I told them about Mable and the old trunk and the trip Tony and I had made to Charleston.

No one spoke. The only sound was the baby gurgling as Teresa and Larry played peek-a-boo with him. I almost laughed out loud. They looked so funny on the floor crawling around.

When Miriam gasped I knew they had reached the part that revealed my identity. Cecil appeared stunned and speechless. Finally, he spoke, "This is the most amazing thing I've ever heard of. The story of a baby born in the water and later disappearing with its mother was strange enough but to discover you, Lilly, were that baby is almost unbelievable."

He continued, "To think you came to Sea Haven looking for me because of my paintings, to the very place of your birth, is incomprehensible. This proves the saying that truth can be stranger than fiction. It sounds like an imaginary story.

"The people of Sea Haven are going to be surprised but happy, as all of us had wondered what happened to Anna and the baby. No one ever heard anything. We were fearful that both of you were dead. It's a happy ending to a mystery we have discussed for years."

"Tony made copies of the letter," I said. "You may keep that copy."

"You must tell old Maudie tomorrow," Cecil said. "She has worried for years speculating about what may have happened."

"Yes, I will visit her early in the morning."

I was up at dawn the next morning and quietly slipped out of bed, closing the door softly so as not to wake Tony. If he heard me he didn't let on. I walked the short distance to the water's edge. There was no doubt now. I knew why I was fascinated with sailboats and schooners and waves washing the shore. I was part of it all. My very being was saturated with a sense of complete wholeness.

Tony didn't have to come get me any more. He knew I needed to be alone from time to time near the water. As I walked back to the lodge I saw Tony waving from the window of our room. I returned a wave. It was a moment of joy and fulfillment never to be forgotten.

We met Larry and Teresa for breakfast in the lodge restaurant.

"Are you going with us to Maudie's?" I asked.

"Teresa wants to go to the General Store first," said Larry.

"We'll meet you later at her house." Teresa continued, "I wonder if Mr. Adkins has another blue moonbeam stone. I would like to have one made into a necklace."

"They're very rare," I said, "but you can inquire."

When Tony and I stepped up on Maudie's porch I could smell the coffee. Her coffee was very bitter and so strong I couldn't drink it.

Maudie had heard we were in Sea Haven and she met us wearing a clean house dress and a freshly starched and ironed apron. Her usual stringy hair was combed and pulled back in a bun. Her wrinkled face bore the traces of a difficult life and the passing of time.

I was so emotional I was trembling and tears were running down my cheeks as I hugged her, realizing what she was about to learn about me.

"Come in," she said. "I'm making doughnuts." Maudie's doughnuts were delicious. They were from an old family recipe.

We followed her to the kitchen and watched as she dropped the cut-out dough into the hot shortening. She knew exactly when to turn them over, and when they were golden brown she lifted them out one by one to drain before dusting them with sugar.

Tony said, "We've had our quota of coffee for today but a glass of milk would be perfect with your doughnuts."

I ate two and Tony ate three as Maudie watched with pride. I didn't know how to begin my story but started with our trip to Charleston.

"My mother's trunk was found in the attic of my old home by a distant cousin and inside was a letter addressed to me and written by my mother.

"Do you want to read it or do you want Tony to read it?" I asked. "I know you have a vision problem."

"You read it, Tony," she said.

We were sitting in her small living room. The windows were up and a gentle breeze was blowing the thin white curtains. The front door was open and a screened door kept out flies and other insects. I could hear the waves as they came ashore, stronger than usual. The ocean seemed to be angry.

Tony had not reached the revealing part of the letter when two children pressed their noses against the screen peering in.

"Aunt Maudie, do you have any doughnuts today?"

"Yes, I do," she said as she got up to unhook the latch of the screened door. "Come in, I have two visitors."

"This is Tony and Lilly." They were adorable children but very shy. I asked, "And what are your names?" They spoke in unison, "Jack and Jill, we're twins and we're four and a half years old."

"Go to the kitchen, children, and you can eat your doughnuts there." Maudie explained that the village children know that she makes doughnuts so they stop by every few days.

Tony continued reading the letter. Every now and then Maudie would say, "Oh, my." When he got to the part of my birth she could hardly contain herself and said, "Land sakes alive." Many old people use this expression when they are surprised but I never did know what it meant.

"Lilly," Maudie said, "I knew when I first met you there was something unusual about you, particularly because you were drawn to the water, but I never dreamed you were the water baby."

Larry and Teresa walked up on the porch and Teresa was very excited. "Mr. Adkins has a blue moonbeam stone and he is going to have it crafted into a necklace. It will take several weeks so he will mail it."

"I'm so happy, Teresa," I said.

Larry introduced Teresa to Maudie and we told them about the doughnuts.

"You may not have any left," Teresa said. "Larry loves doughnuts." We told Maudie we would visit her again before we left Sea Haven.

When we got back to the lodge Joshua was waiting on the porch.

"Laura is sick and Billy wants you to come to their house tomorrow. Will you?"

"Of course, Joshua," I said, "we had planned to visit them before we leave."

We had the restaurant at the lodge prepare a basket of food to take for Laura and Billy. I hoped Laura would be able to eat something.

Billy met us and said, "Momma is in bed but she said all of you can come in." He thanked us for the food and said he thought his mother could eat some of the fruit. Laura was sitting up in bed surrounded by several pillows. She was wearing a turban so I knew she had lost her hair. She looked worse than I expected but she managed a smile.

"Momma," Billy said, "they brought a basket of food. I hope you can eat some of it."

"I hope so too." She turned to Billy. "Take Larry and Tony to the creek and show them the project you're working on."

Laura motioned for me to pull a chair closer to the bed. Teresa sat in a rocker by the window.

"Billy has dropped out of school. I didn't want him to but he insisted. Different women in the village come and help and a nurse from Seattle comes once a week."

"I believe you need more medical attention," I said and Teresa agreed. Teresa added, "I think you should have hospice care. You know about this, don't you?"

"Yes," Laura replied. "In fact the nurse is going to investigate this possibility."

"If you and Billy need anything," I said, "we want to know. Will you promise to have someone call us?"

"Yes, I will," Laura continued. "My greatest concern is Billy. My prognosis is not good. In fact, I may not be able to take any more chemo. I must face this situation realistically."

"Don't worry about Billy," I said. "The four of us will see that he is taken care of and educated. This is a solemn promise."

Laura was crying softly as Teresa and I held her hands. It was evident a great burden had been lifted.

"Now, I have something to tell you," I said. We decided before we reached the house that Laura might not be strong enough to read the letter. I wanted Billy to hear the story so we called the men in from the yard.

I told about the trip to Charleston and the old trunk. Tony was not fully recovered from reading the letter to Maudie the day before. It had been very emotional for him.

"Larry, will you read the letter?" Tony asked.

"Yes, but I think I will condense it. We don't want to tire Laura."

Billy leaned forward, elbows on knees and chin cupped in his hands. The only thing Billy could say was "wow" over and over again. Laura spoke, "Lilly, I felt you were one of us when we first met but I didn't know how or why. This is amazing and wonderful, and finally the mystery has been solved."

We left a copy of the letter so they could read it later. It was hard to say goodbye but we tried to be upbeat. Billy followed us outside. I told him of the promise Teresa and I had made and he smiled, "Larry and Tony have made the same promise. Thank you."

The four of us left Billy standing in the yard watching us. I turned, looked back and ran to him. I hugged him and said, "Don't worry."

"I won't."

It was heart-wrenching to see Billy standing there alone bearing a burden too heavy for one so young. But Laura and Billy were confident they could depend on us and that we would keep our promise.

Chapter 12

We stayed in Sea Haven another day to say good bye. All of the villagers had heard that I was the mysterious water baby and a large crowd had gathered in front of the General Store.

Everyone wanted to shake hands and hug the four of us. A banner held high by a young man read, "You're one of us, Lilly," and a little girl handed me a note that said, "Come back soon."

As we drove away I felt completely drained and I collapsed in Tony's arms. I fell asleep and Tony had to wake me when we reached Seattle.

Our plane was delayed an hour and a half. This gave us time to pull ourselves together.

I was anxious to get back to Canaan, to walk among the flowers, the vineyards and Josie's vegetable garden, to walk with Tony on our beach in the quiet of the evening, to feel the peace and tranquility of Canaan, and also to let him know how much his love and understanding meant to me.

Several weeks passed before I felt rested and more or less back to normal. Laura was on my mind constantly. We kept in touch with Cecil on a weekly basis and he reported that she had some good days but more bad than good.

It was decided that Billy would live with Tony and me when the time came. Teresa was out of town too much to provide a home for a young person. Larry wanted to pay for his education. This seemed to be an equal solution.

Larry was busier than ever with the conservation project. The slogan, "Protect the Earth," had apparently caught the attention of the public and various organizations. It was exciting to drive throughout the city and see the words, "Protect the Earth," painted on the sides of buses and large trucks.

One day while shopping I looked up and saw a dirigible in the sky trailing a banner, "Protect the Earth." The phone in my purse rang; it was Larry. "Where are you, Lilly?"

"On Main Street looking up," I said.

"I was looking out my office window and saw this incredible sight," he said. "I was hoping you were at a place where you could see it."

"Yes, isn't it wonderful? It makes all of our hard work worthwhile."

I was hoping Tony could see this too. I called him and told him to look out the window.

"What is it?"

"Just look out the window."

"I see it, Lilly, I see it. I'm glad you called me."

Larry had one or two speaking engagements a week; he never lost enthusiasm for the subject of conservation so dear to his heart. My schedule was less hectic; I spoke mostly at schools, women's clubs and young men and women's business groups.

Three months after we returned from Sea Haven, Cecil called and said Laura was worse.

"Lilly, Billy wants to know if you can come. The doctor thinks Laura can't last more than a few weeks."

"Yes," I said. "I'll arrange to come in a few days. I need to talk with Tony first."

I suggested that I go alone. Then I would call Tony when the time came and I was sure Larry would come too if possible. Teresa was in Spain and probably wouldn't be back for several weeks.

"I don't like the thought of your going alone," Tony said.

"I'll be fine Tony, really."

He made plane reservations for me and also arranged for a rental car when I reached Seattle.

The days that followed were not as bad as I had anticipated and certainly not as bad as they could have been. Laura was calm and appeared to be at peace. She was in bed most of the time, but occasionally when she was having a better day she wanted to be wheeled to the window where she could see the water and her sailboat anchored in the harbor.

The nurse, Edith, was there full-time, and after I got there I insisted on giving her a break.

"Edith," I said, "you need to get out for awhile, walk on the beach or go to Maudie's; she loves company."

"Are you sure, Lilly?"

"Yes, go, we'll be fine."

Sometimes Laura wanted me to read to her; she was particularly fond of poetry. There were many days when she talked very little, sleeping fitfully.

One day when she was better she asked me to sing to her. I laughed, "I'm not a very good singer, Laura. What do you want me to sing?"

"Two of my favorite hymns," she said. "A hymn book is on the book shelf."

I found the song she wanted and started singing. Edith was in the kitchen cooking and when she heard us she wanted to join in. Billy and Joshua were in the yard and came in to see what was going on. They decided to sing too.

Edith was a large, robust woman who gave the appearance of being stern but as I got to know her I discovered she was very mild mannered and compassionate.

The four of us made a very unlikely quartet. Edith's voice sounded like she was singing bass. I was a mediocre soprano and Joshua was completely off key. Billy was the only one singing very well.

It was very amusing and I almost laughed. If anyone had come by to visit at that time they probably would have thought we were a group of lunatics. But Laura enjoyed it thoroughly and that was the main thing.

As I look back now years later reminiscing I realize that the time I spent with Laura was a beautiful, yet poignant time.

Several days later Laura announced that she wanted to go sailing. I know she missed it as she and Billy usually went sailing every day, but since her illness the sailboat rested forlornly in the harbor.

When she was able to be up in her wheelchair she looked out the window longingly at the waves as they came ashore. I knew the feeling too, so I hoped that Laura could go sailing one more time.

"We'll ask Edith," I said. "I'm not sure."

Edith gave the matter quite a bit of thought and finally said, "We'll go out for a little while. Billy and I will hoist the sails and Lilly can take care of you."

Laura was happier than I had seen her since I had been there. We called Billy in and made arrangements quickly.

It was a beautiful day; the clouds were high, silently floating by as if they were tiptoeing through the sky. The sails went up easily, ready to face the breeze.

There was no conversation. We didn't need to talk. Even Edith, who was known never to be at a loss for words, was silent. Billy's countenance gave the appearance of a contented young fellow as he skillfully maneuvered the boat sailing along without a sound.

Laura slipped her frail hand in mine and we smiled. We were in communication in a way that transcended all understanding. This was another mountain-top experience that I recalled many years later.

I didn't want the day to end but we had been out long enough. I could sense that Laura was getting tired.

Edith spoke first, "It's time to go home, Billy."

Laura was getting weaker each day and I felt that the end was near. I thought to myself that I needed to talk with Billy but I didn't know what to say.

Late one afternoon I told Edith I wanted to walk on the beach if she didn't need me to do something for Laura.

"Go," she said. "You look like you could use a break."

Billy was reading or studying stretched out on the ground under a big tree.

"Billy, come walk with me."

"Sea Haven will always hold a special place in my heart," I said. "It was my first home and it's so peaceful and beautiful. But you and I will have to leave soon, Billy. I don't think your mother will last much longer."

"No, I don't think so either. Momma says I must look on the bright side and be thankful that you, Tony and Larry want to take care of me." He was crying now and I took his hand; I didn't know whether he wanted me to hug him or not. I motioned toward a bench which had been placed near the water's edge for old folks to sit.

He broke down and sobbed in my arms. "It's all right to cry, Billy. Men need to express their emotions as well as women. It has nothing to do with your manhood."

Laura was sleeping most of the time but early one morning she aroused and motioned for me to come to her bed. She took my hand and acted as though she wanted to tell me something. Her lips were moving but there was no sound; I leaned closer and she whispered, "Talk to Maudie."

I told Billy I thought he should sit with his mother and I left the room. Edith said there was nothing left to do.

A few hours passed and Billy came to my room. "Momma's gone. I must go ring the bell in the church tower. It is only rung when someone dies or does not return from the sea."

Now at this fleeting moment in time I thought that someone must have rung the bell when my father did not return from the sea.

Laura's funeral was simple and beautiful. She had requested that anyone who wanted to speak should do so.

Cecil spoke first. He told of her quiet and gentle spirit. Mr. Adkins said, "Laura was a woman of fairness, honesty and integrity."

I asked Tony and Larry to stand on each side of me as we got up to speak. I needed physical support to get through this. As I looked into the faces of the audience gathered in this small village church I knew I was looking into the faces of the best people in the world—people whose simple philosophy was honesty, compassion, love of their fellowman and trust in God.

Joshua was sitting with Billy giving him the only support he knew how to give—his presence.

Larry and Tony related again how the three of us came to know Laura. Larry told of our first visit to Sea Haven when we came to find Cecil. Tony told of our subsequent trips and how the three of us learned to love the village and its people. He mentioned Maudie's hospitality and everyone's friendliness.

Now it was my turn and I was crying softly but I wanted to speak.

"Sea Haven will always be a special place to me. I was born in the waters here that you can see from the windows of this building. You are my people and I love each and every one of you.

"We are going to take Billy with us when we leave in a few days, but we'll be back as often as possible. Billy is a bright and intelligent young man and Larry, Tony and I want him to have the very best education. Most of you know that he is very interested in oceanography and the university that specializes in this field is located outside Santa Barbara. We discussed our plans with Laura and she was in agreement. She also signed legal papers designating Tony and Larry co-guardians and I was appointed Power of Attorney."

I motioned for Billy to join us on the platform. Larry spoke, "We promise you in front of these witnesses that we will fulfill the rights, privileges and responsibilities in the same manner as if you were our biological son."

There was no sound except what goes along with crying; there wasn't a dry eye. I couldn't help but think that Laura would be pleased with her unusual funeral. The silence was broken when Edith stood and in her untrained, bass-like voice started singing "Amazing Grace." It was the most beautiful singing I had ever heard.

Billy was about to face the unknown but he was brave and felt secure. I think he had prepared himself as much as a young person has the capacity to in this kind of situation. He had never been far from home, only to Seattle and Tacoma.

It had been difficult to leave Sea Haven and the wonderful people. I will never be able to erase from my memory the scene of Joshua standing by Billy and looking so forlorn. But Cecil told Joshua he could go with him the next time he goes to Santa Barbara taking paintings to the Art Gallery.

Chapter 13

The first thing we needed to do was find out where Billy stood academically. A very good private school, Highland Academy, was not far from Canaan, so I contacted the Headmaster there.

"Bring Billy in next Tuesday for testing," said Dr. Manley. "I'll look forward to meeting you, Mrs. Saunders, and later I want to meet your husband also."

The testing was extensive and took two days. Billy's IQ was above average and in some areas was superior. Dr. Manley was very pleased with the results. Billy would be placed in the 12th grade, one and a half grade levels above what his age indicated.

The door opened and a very attractive middle-aged woman entered.

"Mrs. Saunders, Billy, this is Dr. Agnes Brown. She is one of our administrators and also serves as a counselor." Dr. Manley continued, "Billy, Dr. Brown would like to give you a tour of the school, meet some of the teachers and students, and also find out about your interests."

This gave me an opportunity to tell Billy's story. In order to bring out all the facts it was necessary for me to start at the beginning when Larry and I went to Sea Haven and the purpose of this trip.

Dr. Manley was very attentive and when I finished he said, "What an amazing story! Billy is a very fortunate young lad."

"We feel that we are fortunate to have this opportunity to make a difference in Billy's life," I said. "It works both ways you know."

Billy and Dr. Brown were back from their tour. I knew from his expression it had gone well.

"Lilly," Billy said, "I have my assignments for Thursday and a list of books to get."

"Good," I said, "where do we get the books?"

"The book store is only open on Mondays and Thursdays," Dr. Brown said. "Billy can get them Thursday and here is the name of the store that sells our uniforms."

Billy and I had noticed when we arrived at Highland how neatly the students were dressed. The school colors were navy blue and burgundy, a dark red.

Tony and I had been apprehensive about how Billy would adapt to his new life in a strange place and meeting new people. We need not have worried at least so far. He was enthusiastic about everything. He liked Alexander and Josie and they liked him. He said we had described Canaan and Promised Land so well that it was just as he had pictured.

Billy woke us up early Wednesday morning ready to go shopping. Tony was going with us. He was anxious to see Billy in his new clothes.

"What time is it?" Tony asked sleepily.

"It's six," Billy said.

"The shop isn't open yet," I said. "It's not like the General Store in Sea Haven that opens at five o'clock to sell supplies to the fishermen. We'll have to wait until ten o'clock."

"I'm going to walk on the beach," Billy said. I suggested he go back to bed but he said he was too excited to sleep. "Josie works in her vegetable garden early in the morning. You can visit her after you take a walk."

When Billy walks on the beach I know he's thinking about Laura. I don't usually join him because I know he needs the time alone.

Our usual breakfast time was 8:00 or 8:30. I had just gone into the kitchen to get a glass of orange juice when I looked through the window and saw Billy and Josie coming through the gate that separates Canaan from Promised Land. They were in a deep conversation and I could see a bond was forming between them.

Tony came to the window and I said, "Look, Tony." I'm not sure but I think I saw a tear or two almost ready to fall. He kissed me and one of my tears fell on his face. It was another moment I wish I could hold onto forever.

I had experienced so many moments that I wish I could keep and maybe relive. I guess I should write a book—maybe I will sometime.

Billy's new wardrobe consisted of navy blue pants, burgundy jacket and tie, white shirt, also a burgundy sweater. When we got home he raced into the house to find Josie and show her his clothes.

"My, aren't you going to be the handsome one, Billy," Josie said. "Look out world, here comes Billy."

These were happy days for all of us. Billy was eager to learn and he was appreciative of everything we gave him and all that was being done for him.

Tony was teaching Billy to play tennis. They went to the club every Saturday morning. It was evident the bond was growing stronger between them. Larry preferred golf. He and Tony had played together regularly for years, long before I met either one of them. When time and schedules permitted Larry took Billy golfing and often the three went together.

If it was inconvenient for me to pick up Billy from school, Alexander was more than willing to get him. Billy was inquisitive about everything. He followed Alexander around as he worked in the vineyard asking dozens of questions regarding planting and growing of trees, flowers and shrubs.

But I wasn't neglected. Billy talked to me about serious matters, seeking advice about many things. We were becoming closer and I hoped I would have the wisdom to guide him in the right way.

He liked one girl in particular at school and he didn't know if she liked him. This was a new experience for Billy and he didn't know how to act.

"Does she talk to you and is she friendly?" I asked.

"Yes, but she's nice to everybody."

"Just be yourself, don't appear overly anxious but still show interest. Continue to talk and in time you'll know whether or not she likes you."

"Thanks, Lilly, you're great."

One day, quite unexpectedly, Billy called Tony "Dad." I don't think he was aware of saying it and Tony was caught off guard. He didn't want to react in a noticeable way but he was visibly moved. He put his hand on Billy's shoulder.

One day about two weeks later when I picked up Billy at school he said, "Lilly, I've told everybody at school that I have two dads, Tony and Larry. Is that all right?"

"Of course, it is. If you feel this way about them, I think it's wonderful."

"My friends think it's neat."

"Sure, it is."

We stopped in the driveway at home but Billy didn't get out immediately.

"Lilly."

"Yes, Billy."

"Is it OK if I continue to call you 'Lilly?'"

"Yes, I don't expect you to call me 'Mom.' You had a mother but you didn't know your father. It doesn't hurt my feelings at all."

He hopped out of the car. "Thanks, Lilly." He raced across the lawn looking for Alexander.

I didn't get out of the car immediately. "Wow," I thought, "these mountain-top moments come when you least expect it, but what a joy!"

Tony and I enjoyed being Billy's parents. Dr. Manley asked us to be sponsors for the senior class and we attended many of the school activities. Larry came when he could and Teresa also came part of the time.

Teresa was not traveling as much as usual and I mentioned it to Larry.

"She hasn't been feeling well and decided to cut back on the travels."

I didn't think she looked good but I didn't say anything.

"Has she been to the doctor?" I asked.

"Yes, he's running tests."

One day just as Billy and I were coming in from school, Josie ran out to the car and said that Cecil was on the phone. He was planning to come next Wednesday, four days away, and Joshua was coming with him.

"We want you to stay with us," I said, "and bring Miriam and Joseph."

"Miriam thinks the trip would be too hard for them but plans to come later when Joseph is older and can enjoy the trip."

Billy was very excited and began making plans to entertain Joshua.

It was late afternoon when their plane got in. It was Joshua's first plane trip and he was talking non-stop.

Billy wanted Cecil and Joshua to see the vineyard and Josie's vegetable garden first thing. For awhile it was chaos and finally Tony decided it was time for the boys to get quiet.

"All right, boys, it's time to settle down. There will be plenty of time for you to do all the things you've planned."

Cecil planned to take his paintings to the Art Gallery the next day, and Tony told Billy and Joshua if they didn't want to go he would plan something for them to do.

"No," said Joshua, "I want to go back to Sea Haven and tell everybody that I went to the Art Gallery and saw Cecil's paintings on the wall."

Jack was glad to see us and said, "Cecil, all of your paintings have sold and I have a check for you."

"Good, I've brought more. Do you think you can sell them?"

"I'm sure of it. You are beginning to be recognized as an outstanding painter. You'll probably be famous one of these days."

Larry called and wanted us to come for dinner on Saturday night.

"Larry," I said, "as Teresa is not feeling well, I think it would be too much work for her."

"No, she has insisted. Naomi and Peter will make all the preparations and Teresa can supervise."

Larry and Teresa's home was very different from Canaan. It was called Villa of Eden, usually referred to as Eden. The only similarity was that it was on the ocean but the house set back farther and the beach was smaller.

The house was Mediterranean style and very beautiful. Teresa had a distinct flair for decorating. She should have been an interior designer.

Many of the furnishings were purchased in the various countries she had visited but the most interesting thing about Eden was the gardens—several mini-gardens representing different cultures.

The Japanese garden was formal with small trees and shrubs shaped in the bonsai style and a pond of bright colored fish and a waterfall. The Persian garden had many flowers with large blossoms indigenous to that part of the world. There was an English garden and a wild flower garden and one of the prettiest was the Dutch garden with tulips of every color.

Twice a year tours were sponsored by the Pacific Coast Horticultural Society and the price of admission was donated to "Protect the Earth, Inc."

Lee was the gardener and he took great pride in maintaining the gardens to perfection and he was very enthusiastic during the tours as he liked to answer the many questions that were asked.

Larry had told us to come early so Cecil and the boys could see the gardens before dark. Joshua had so many questions I was afraid Lee would get tired but he seemed to enjoy every minute.

Naomi was the cook and housekeeper and Peter called himself "the Handy Man." His duties were varied and numerous. They lived in a charming cottage on the property that looked like it came out of a fairy tale book.

After dinner Billy and Joshua walked down to the beach. Their friendship was amazing; even though miles apart intellectually they possessed a rapport that many of us might envy.

Joshua knew he was limited and not as smart as Billy but it did not affect his self-esteem. In fact at times he got carried away and acted like he was running the village of Sea Haven. But everyone loved Joshua and he added local color that helped make Sea Haven unique.

I thought this was a good time to tell Larry and Teresa about my conversation with Maudie after Laura's death. Tony and I had been so busy since Billy came to live with us that there hadn't been an opportunity to talk.

Maudie told me this story the day we left Sea Haven to bring Billy home with us. Maudie was showing her age and her voice cracked occasionally as she talked.

"Laura and Marshall Evans came to Sea Haven a short time after they married. Marshall worked in a factory in a small town nearby and Laura did beautiful embroidered hand work to supplement their income. Mr. Adkins told Laura she could display her embroidered pillow cases at the General Store.

"Three years later Billy was born and with another person to feed and clothe Marshall tried to get a better job, but things were kinda slow everywhere and he couldn't find any other work.

"When Billy was almost three Marshall told Laura he was going away for a few days to look for work farther down the coast."

Maudie stopped to sip the lemonade we were drinking on her porch and I could tell she was affected emotionally. She went on, "Two days passed and Marshall called but seemed dejected. He said he wanted to look some more and would call again in a few days, but Marshall never came home.

"Two weeks later Laura received a letter. It read:

'Dear Laura,

I'm so sorry but I won't be back. The responsibility is too great. I will try to send some money from time to time. I'm too ashamed to face you because I can't provide for you and Billy at this time. Please forgive me.

Signed - Marshall.'"

I could hardly believe what Maudie was telling me and it made me very sad. I said, "Is that the end of the story?"

"No, not quite. Three weeks later she received a check for $100 but no message. Every month a check came but the amounts varied and the postmarks were from different cities.

"About a year later a check for $5000 came mailed from Los Angeles. A note said, 'I've saved this for you and Billy. I'm leaving the United States and not sure where I will go. Again, I'm sorry.' Laura never heard from him after that and no more money came."

As I finished the story Larry and Teresa looked stunned. Cecil said he had already heard bits and pieces that confirmed what I had related as told to me by Maudie.

Joshua and Cecil left the next day to return home. We promised we would come to Sea Haven in a few months if possible.

Chapter 14

We settled into our regular routine and the time went by quickly. Teresa was not any better. Larry was seeking medical help on the Internet. Teresa's doctor was almost certain she had a bacterial infection but was unable to locate the source. It had been suggested that they contact medical research teams who might be able to identify the bacteria.

Billy was happy in school and finally had the courage to ask Iris to one of the school's activities. I did not know her, and suggested to Billy I would like to meet her. He said Highland was having a get acquainted party for parents, teachers and students in a few weeks.

"Great," I said, "Tony and I will come and meet everyone and maybe we can invite Iris and her parents to visit us, that is, if you want to."

"Oh yes, I would like that very much."

In the meantime Larry had some encouraging news. A medical team in Chicago had seen Larry's request on the Internet seeking information regarding Teresa's symptoms. Two doctors there had been successful in diagnosing difficult cases of bacterial infections, and they told Larry to bring Teresa to Chicago immediately.

Tony and I took Larry and Teresa to the airport. Billy was in school. They were prepared to stay indefinitely and I was going to look after Larry's office with the help of his long-time, very efficient secretary.

"I'll call every few days," I said, "and keep you posted."

Billy almost drove us crazy before the "Highland Get-Acquainted Night" came. He was so excited. It was a new experience for him so we tried to be patient. He wanted to get there early before Iris and her parents arrived, for what reason I didn't know.

I could see right away why Billy liked her. Iris was tall, just a few inches shorter than Billy; she had dark brown hair, almost black, and the darkest blue eyes I had ever seen. Her parents, Tim and Nan Gallagher, were very attractive and nice. The evening was enjoyable and Billy was a most happy fellow.

It was three days before we heard from Larry.

"We've rented a small apartment in the medical complex," he said. "It's near the research center which is a part of the hospital."

The doctors wanted Teresa to remain in the hospital while they ran extensive tests. They were optimistic they would be able to pinpoint the source of infection.

I went by Larry's office three times a week to check on things but the secretary, Cornelia, assured me that everything was fine.

Billy came in from school one day and said that all moms were invited to have lunch with their children the following Monday.

"Will you come, Lilly?"

"Of course, I'll come. I would like to."

Nan Gallagher was there and I enjoyed visiting with her again and also meeting some new mothers at the school.

Billy wanted me to meet some of his friends I hadn't seen before. He introduced me as his mom. This was the first time he had referred to me as his mother and I felt a sense of joy not previously experienced. Surely my cup was overflowing.

It was also time to think about where Billy would go to college. He was still interested in oceanography but due to Larry's influence he was also interested in other phases of conservation.

Dr. Brown called me one day. "Mrs. Saunders, I need to talk with you and your husband about college plans for Billy."

"Yes, we want to do that soon but we must wait until Larry Mathis gets back from Chicago. He's with his wife there while she goes through testing for an unusual bacterial infection."

"Oh, I'm so sorry, I didn't know."

"We're hoping the research team will find an effective medication soon. We'll make an appointment with you as soon as Mr. Mathis returns."

Three weeks later Larry called, "The doctors have found a medicine they believe will help Teresa. And Lilly, the strange thing is that the extract comes from a plant and through herbs that grow in the rain forest where we were stationed."

"I'm so glad," I said. "It sounds very promising."

The days and weeks flew by and everything seemed to be running smoothly. Larry called and reported that the injections were gradually helping in a remarkable way. Teresa's appetite had improved and her energy level was up.

"If this continues," Larry said, "the doctors have said maybe we can come home and Teresa will receive the injections at a local hospital."

"Wonderful!" I said. "This is good news. Tony and I miss both of you and Billy does too."

On Friday afternoon when I picked up Billy at school, he was not his usual jovial self. Although he liked school he looked forward to the weekend when Tony played tennis with him.

"What's wrong, Billy?" I said. I had never seen him like this.

"The prom is coming up in two weeks," he said dejectedly. "Iris wants to go and I don't know how to dance."

This brought back memories of my own youth and my heart ached for him. When you're young many things are traumatic which in later life seem trivial compared to life's trials and tribulations.

"What did you tell Iris?"

"I was very embarrassed but I told her the truth."

"Was she upset?" I asked.

"No, just surprised I think, and she said, 'Get your mom or dad to teach you. It's very easy.'"

"Lilly, would you teach me to dance?"

"I'm not very good but I know someone who will be a good teacher."

"Who?"

"Josie, she's a very good dancer."

"Really?"

"Yes, we'll get started tonight. It will be lots of fun."

"I'm not too sure," Billy said. He hesitated, then gave me a hug. "Thanks, Mom."

Sometimes he called me "Lilly" and sometimes "Mom." I gladly settled for either one. When we got home Josie was in the kitchen stringing green beans fresh from her garden.

I said, "Can you put the dinner preparations on hold? Billy wants to ask you something."

"Sure, what is it?"

Shyly, he said, "Will you teach me to dance?"

"Well, now," Josie replied, "so you want to learn to dance?"

"Yes, the school prom is two weeks from now and Iris wants to go."

"I've about got these beans ready to cook and when I get them on, we'll start," said Josie. "Alexander is in the yard, Billy, tell him to come in and move some of the furniture in the living room."

The room had area rugs which could be rolled up.

I was in charge of the music and things were in full swing when Tony appeared at the door.

"What's going on?" he asked. "I heard the music from the driveway."

"Billy's learning to dance so he can take Iris to the school prom."

"Well, how about that," Tony said, as he grabbed me and whirled me around the room.

The following week we received sad news. Cecil called to say that Maudie died a few days ago.

"A fisherman found her on the porch as he was going to his schooner about five o'clock in the morning. She had gone to her final sleep while drinking coffee. The cup had fallen to the floor."

"I'm so sorry," I said. "Maudie was special. She was very kind to me."

Cecil continued, "She had made doughnuts the day before and several of the children had visited her. They are very upset. As soon as Joshua heard the news he ran to the church to ring the bell in the tower."

Cecil said everything else was going well in Sea Haven. Joseph was growing and was quite a handful, keeping Miriam busy.

"Cecil," I asked, "do you think you could paint a picture of Maudie sitting on her porch looking out over the water?"

"I don't know, Lilly. I thought about it at one time but never got around to it."

Tony and Billy were saddened to hear the news and we told Josie and Alexander what a colorful character Old Maudie had been.

The good news was that Larry and Teresa were coming home. She was much better. The medication was killing the deadly bacteria and the doctors said she could receive the injections in Los Angeles at a clinic that specialized in uncommon infections. Fortunately they had access to the medication.

Billy had not applied for a driver's license. He was old enough and Tony taught him to drive but Billy was a little apprehensive, not being familiar with the city and surrounding areas. He didn't appear to be in a hurry and we certainly didn't push him.

Iris had been driving two years so she insisted on picking up Billy for the prom. She came in and we watched proudly as he nervously pinned the corsage on her shoulder. We took pictures, of course, and told them we would see them later as Tony and I had been asked to be chaperones.

Teresa looked surprisingly well and she said she felt almost like her old self. Larry, Tony and I made an appointment with Dr. Brown to discuss Billy's continued education after high school. He was still interested in oceanography but also wanted to study conservation, due to Larry's influence and mine.

Dr. Brown said that she thought a college in San Diego offered courses in both of these subjects.

"I know one of the administrators there. I'll call now." Dr. Smithfield was in his office and said he would like to meet Billy, so we made an appointment for the following Wednesday.

Teresa decided not to make the trip to San Diego.

"I think that's a wise decision, Teresa," I said. "You need to rest."

At first we thought we would drive to San Diego but the more we thought about it we decided to fly. It was over two hundred miles and we could save time by flying. Billy was definitely in favor of flying.

The campus was beautiful, overlooking the ocean, and the name of the college was very appropriate. The grounds were landscaped to perfection, and plants, trees and flowers were everywhere. We later discovered they had working gardens where students practiced what they were learning.

Pacific College of Conservation and Oceanography had an enrollment of only 1200 but it had a very high academic rating and we also thought that Billy would do better in a small college.

As soon as we opened the door Larry saw a man he had gone to college with.

"Hi, Daniel Davis," he said.

"Larry Mathis, what are you doing here? I saw your documentary and was very impressed."

He looked at me and said, "And I recognize you."

"Yes," Larry said, "this is Lilly, my business partner and her husband, Tony Saunders."

"And who is this young man?"

"This is Billy," Larry said. "We are his guardians and he is interested in attending school here."

Daniel was one of the professors and he said J. T. Martin was also on the faculty.

"J. T.?" Larry said. "I wondered what happened to him."

Daniel introduced us to Dr. Smithfield and he took us on a tour of the grounds, the class rooms and the labs. We stayed so long we decided to stay over until the next day.

It was six months until high school graduation so we needed to get things worked out for college as soon as possible.

Billy liked everything about Pacific U. (this is what the students called it). Everyone seemed to like Billy as he was very personable and enthusiastic, and never met a stranger.

Chapter 15

The days, weeks, months and years went flying by. Nathanael visited often and was married now. His wife's name was Amanda and we liked her very much. Nathanael's degree was in marine biology and he worked for the Government Marine Laboratories.

Billy was ready to graduate and was going to work for Larry at Conservation Foundation. Larry's enthusiasm had rubbed off on him. He would be a good advocate for "Protect the Earth."

Billy and Iris were engaged and planned to be married after he was settled on his job.

Tony was looking unusually tired and seemed to have less energy than normal. I talked him into seeing his doctor. Extensive testing revealed a small artery blockage to the heart.

"What can be done?" I asked.

"The balloon procedure may work as there is no apparent heart damage."

Tony agreed to the procedure, which surprised me. He must have been feeling worse than I thought.

Everything went well and we left the hospital in a few days with a number of instructions.

"Here's your diet, Tony," he said, handing him a list, "and this is your exercise chart. Also, I want you to cut back on your work load."

"This isn't going to be easy," Tony said.

"No, I know," the doctor said, "but it's very important for you to follow these rules."

Tony was a better patient than I thought he might be.

When Billy came to live with us, Tony and I decided we would leave Canaan to him and we put this in a will to that effect.

Billy and Iris were married on a late September day in a small rural church. He wanted Larry and Tony both to stand up with him, and as I sat on the front row reserved for mother of the groom, I was unable to keep back the tears.

Across the aisle Nan Gallagher was in tears also as we watched Iris walk down the aisle slowly on her father's arm. I'm sure we had the same feeling, "Surely our cup overflowed with joy and spilled into the saucer."

Cecil, Miriam, Joseph and Joshua came to the wedding. Joseph was a big boy, already in school. He hung on to Joshua much to his delight. Joshua was playing the big brother role.

We told Billy and Iris they could live with us at Canaan. "There's plenty of room," Tony said, but they decided to live nearby in a small cottage for awhile.

Two years later Nathanael and Amanda had a baby girl and they named her Lilly Ann. No grandmother has ever been more proud.

Three and a half years later Billy and Iris had a baby boy named Anthony Laurence. Tony and Larry were almost unbearable to be around they were so proud.

Tony decided to retire but retained ownership of the company and remained chairman of the board. I thought he might get restless but he seemed very content. He spent time with Alexander in the vineyard and helped Josie in the garden. He and Billy played tennis about twice a month and he and Larry played golf occasionally.

Every now and then the thought crossed my mind that Tony could have a heart attack sometime. I knew I needed to be realistic.

I could not bear the thought of ever living without Tony. He was my knight in shining armor. At the time in my life when I knew it was necessary to set aside my feelings for Larry, Tony came to my rescue. No man could have been more wonderful to a woman than Tony had been to me. He was good, strong, understanding, compassionate and loving; he also had a sense of humor. He loved Billy like a son and was the most unselfish man I had ever known.

Was Tony perfect? No, no human is; but at that moment I couldn't think of a fault I could name.

One morning when we had been married twelve years, Tony woke up with chest pains. He called me, "Lilly, I hate to wake you but I have a few chest pains."

"I'll call the doctor," I said. My heart was pounding but I knew I must stay as calm as possible. Alexander and Josie were still at their house and I told them to dress and come over.

The doctor said to bring Tony in. By that time Tony said he was feeling some better.

"But we need to have you checked," I said.

The doctor was waiting at his office when we arrived even though it was too early for office hours.

He checked Tony thoroughly and said, "I think he should be admitted to the hospital as a precaution."

The day was spent in testing and I knew Tony was exhausted but he wanted to talk. The doctor wanted him to remain overnight and I said I was staying also.

The room had a sofa that made into a bed. Alexander and Josie decided to stay in the lounge down the hall. Tony drifted off to sleep and I was dozing. Two hours later he called me.

"Lilly, I'm afraid I haven't told you often enough that I love you."

"Tony, you've told me every day for more than twelve years and sometimes more than once a day."

"I never knew anyone could make me as happy as you have," he said.

"Save your energy, Tony, and go to sleep. We'll talk in the morning."

"I love you, Lilly."

"I love you, too, Tony."

An hour later the nurse came in to take his vital signs. I woke up and noticed she was upset. She called "Code Blue" and several doctors and nurses came in. I was in shock and numb. Then the doctor came to me and said, "He's gone, he died in his sleep peacefully."

The next few hours were a blur. The doctor insisted I take a mild medication and I refused at first but finally decided the pain of sorrow was almost too hard to bear.

WHEN THE SAILS GO UP AND THE WAVES COME ASHORE

Alexander and Josie got me in the car but I felt numb and out of touch. Larry and Teresa were at Canaan when we got home; Billy and Iris were there too. Larry was in a terrible shape. He and Tony had been best friends since high school. Alexander got word to Nathanael and Amanda and they came.

Everyone insisted that I lie down for awhile and I was so exhausted, plus the medicine, that I fell asleep.

We decided the funeral would be at the church where Billy and Iris got married. Billy said he was sure it had a bell tower and for some reason he wanted the bell rung seven times.

Cecil, Miriam and Joshua came; a friend kept Joseph. Mr. Adkins came and I couldn't believe how frail he was. Recent years had taken a heavy toll on him. Jack from the Art Gallery was also there.

Billy found an old man who repaired the rusty bell and at the appointed time the bell tolled seven times. This seemed to give Billy some kind of comfort and peace, and to me it was a symbol of the passing from life to death.

I knew I had to carry on but there were days I didn't want to live. During those times I walked on the beach and watched the waves come ashore and imagined the schooners hoisting their sails at Sea Haven.

It was on a beach that Tony and I shared our love for the first time. And we realized we wanted to spend our lives together. Our life together had been wonderful but cut short far too soon, and I was left barren with only my memories to sustain me.

Everyone around me tried to comfort me and I tried to be brave especially for Billy's sake. He had lost a father. He and Tony had grown so close. Iris was a big help. She had an unusual soothing power on Billy and also on me. I was amazed at her maturity and thought to myself what a good choice Billy had made.

Several weeks after the funeral Iris announced that she was pregnant. Anthony was going to have a sibling.

Four months after Tony's death I decided I wanted to go to Sea Haven.

"Billy, can you go with me to Sea Haven for a few days?"

"I don't know, Mom, I would like to but I'll have to check with Larry. I don't know if he has something I need to take care of."

Larry said it was fine for us to go. Iris couldn't go on account of her pregnancy and also taking care of Anthony.

Billy made all of the arrangements. I was so proud of Billy. He had matured rapidly and was a self assured, responsible young man. I didn't worry about any of the details.

He called Cecil and he made reservations for us at the Lodge. When we reached Seattle we got a rental car and Billy drove to Sea Haven.

My mind drifted back to that early autumn day many years ago when Larry and I made the first trip to Sea Haven in search of the artist, Cecil. So many things had happened, so many people had entered our lives. Some had come and now gone—Laura, Nathanael's father, Luke, Old Maudie and now Tony, a father to Billy and a beloved husband to me.

Billy was silent most of the way. I knew he was thinking of Laura, his boyhood days, and his friendship with Joshua, when young boys dreamed of the future and days were carefree.

Billy called Cecil as soon as we checked in at the Lodge. Joshua answered the phone.

"We're expecting you for dinner. Come on now."

Joshua had made a place for himself in the world. In spite of his limitations he was a person of worth. Ever since he could walk he ran errands for everyone in Sea Haven, and recently the people had appointed him honorary village Marshall. He was one of the happiest people I had ever met and his aim was to serve others. All of us could learn a lot from Joshua.

The next day Billy and Joshua wanted to go off together. I imagine they were going to the cemetery, to the church and Laura's old house.

"Mom, will you be all right?"

"Oh sure, I'll be fine. I'm going to the General Store to visit, then to the beach."

I was disappointed when I reached the General Store. Mr. Adkins was not well and was at home. His son Ed was running the business.

Ed was grown now; I remembered him as a small boy always getting in his father's way.

Ed knew me. "Ah, Lilly, Sea Haven's water baby. How are you?"

"I'm a very sad woman, Ed, my husband died four months ago and I miss him so much."

"Oh yes, Cecil told all of us about Mr. Tony. I'm so sorry."

"Does anyone live in Maudie's house?" I asked.

"Yes, a fisherman and his daughter, Rachel. Go down and meet Miss Rachel. You'll like her."

Rachel was sitting on the porch. The house had been painted and looked much better.

"Rachel, I'm Lilly." Before I could finish she said, "Yes, I know who you are, come in."

She continued, "Dad and I moved to Sea Haven shortly after you and your husband took Billy. I'm so glad to meet you. Maudie told me about you and the amazing story of your birth. You're special here in Sea Haven."

"And Sea Haven is special to me," I said. "This is my home and the villagers are like family."

"By the way," Rachel said, "Maudie gave me her doughnut recipe. I just made a fresh batch. Come inside and have one with a cup of coffee." I almost laughed thinking how terrible Maudie's coffee was. Rachel's coffee was delicious and the doughnuts tasted the same.

"I want to walk on the beach before Billy gets back," I said. "I'll visit you again when I come to Sea Haven."

"See that you do just that," she said. She stood on the porch watching me and I turned to wave.

The beach was the same. The schooners and fishermen were out of sight—a few sailboats were lazily drifting along taking their passengers on a tranquil ride over the water where cares and sorrows melt away.

The waves still rolled ashore in the same rhythmic pattern as always. The fishermen brought their schooners in at dusk and the next day it will be the same.

That night when we got back to the Lodge, Billy called Iris to see if she was all right. She was fine.

"I'll see you day after tomorrow. Tell Anthony 'Hi' from Daddy. I love you, Iris."

Tony had been a good influence on Billy. He noticed the day he came to live with us that Tony told me several times a day that he loved me. It was heart-warming now to hear him say the same words to his wife.

"Call Larry, Billy, and see how things are at the office."

"Hi, Dad, how are things at work? Good. We'll be in day after tomorrow. Are you going to pick us up? See you then. Do you want to talk with Lilly?"

"Hi, Larry."

"How's everything in Sea Haven?" he asked.

"Everything has changed. Mr. Adkins is not well. His son, Ed, is running the store. Someone is living in Laura's house. I don't know who. Maudie's house has been painted and a fisherman and his daughter live there.

"The only thing not changed is the beach, the water and the waves coming ashore on time; the schooners go out at five in the morning and the sailboats are in the same position."

"Things have to change, Lilly, even though we don't like it. It would be a stagnant world otherwise."

"I guess so," I said. "See you Thursday."

"Goodnight, Lilly."

Larry and I had not talked since Tony's death. We couldn't because both of us were grieving, each in a different way. He was grieving for his best friend since high school and I for my beloved husband.

Billy and Iris decided to move to Canaan. They were outgrowing their cottage.

"Mom, is the offer still good for us to live at Canaan?"

"Of course," I said. "I was hoping you would decide to make your home here. The house is so large and I'm very lonely without Tony. Josie and I can help with the children."

I was now the owner of Tony's company, "Saunders Projections," and I wasn't sure what I wanted to do with it. One thing I was sure of, I didn't want to run a business, as I was still involved with "Protect the Earth." I discussed the matter with Tony's attorney and financial adviser and so far I wasn't impressed with any of their proposals.

I asked Billy if he was interested.

"I'm sorry, Lilly, but I prefer working with Larry on conservation projects."

"I understand, Billy, but I wanted to give you an opportunity just in case."

I thought I should talk with Larry about this but I had delayed until both of us felt better. Shortly before Tony's death Larry had been discussing another trip to a remote part of the world to gather information pertinent to conservation.

I decided to call Larry. "Hi, Larry."

"Hi, Lilly, how are you?"

"I'm OK. What about you?"

"I'm OK too. What's on your mind?"

"Can you meet me for lunch? I want to discuss business matters."

"Sure, where and when?"

"Henri's at 12:30?"

"Make it 1:15. I have a meeting that may run overtime."

"Fine, see you at 1:15."

Larry got there before I did and had a table in a quiet spot where we could talk. "My meeting ended sooner than I thought," he said.

I jumped into what I had in mind. "I know you have been planning to visit some of the conservation troubled spots. Do you have any plans now?"

"Yes, and I was going to tell you about these plans soon. I wanted to take Billy with me, but now that Iris is pregnant, I'm sure he wouldn't want to leave her at this time."

"How long did you plan to be gone?"

"Four or five weeks."

"Do you think you could wait until after the baby comes? I think it is important that Billy see firsthand the erosion and destruction of the earth."

"I do too. Billy has surprised me with his enthusiasm and

conscientiousness, and he is very valuable to our organization. I've waited this long, I can wait until things settle down after the new baby comes."

"Good. Another matter I want to discuss. I'm now the owner of 'Saunders Projections' and I don't know what to do with it. I don't want to run it as I don't feel capable and also I'm committed to 'Protect the Earth.'

"Also I like the role of grandmother and want to help Billy and Iris with the children. Josie is a big help too."

"Do you want to sell the company?" asked Larry.

"I was hoping you might want to buy it," I said.

"Wow! I don't think I can afford the amount of money the company is worth. However, it would be valuable as we would not have to pay camera crews for production of short subjects and documentaries."

"Exactly my thought."

Then Larry flashed that beautiful smile that had gotten my attention when we first met and I had not seen in a long time, and he said, "Lilly, what else is going on in your head? I know your wheels are spinning."

I smiled—he knew me too well. Larry had always been able to read my mind to a certain extent.

"Yes, I do have another proposal. Would you consider a partnership? You would buy 48% of the company, I would retain 52% and you could have the option to purchase my 52% at any time. Andy Zanier would remain as manager. He's reliable. Tony always had complete confidence in him."

"This is very interesting. Did you come up with this idea yourself?"

"Of course I did," I said, slightly annoyed.

"You never cease to amaze me, Lilly."

I never know what to say when people say this to me. I don't really know what they mean. I usually don't respond.

Larry continued, "I'll have to consult my banker, financial adviser and Teresa."

"No hurry, I know a decision of this magnitude requires careful consideration."

"Yes, it does."

Chapter 16

Billy and Iris knew the baby was a girl so they were shopping accordingly. Iris and Nan shopped together and they asked me to join them but I declined. I thought they should shop alone.

Several times Iris asked me to go alone with her and I appreciated her thoughtfulness. She was a wise young woman beyond her years.

Larry told Billy of his plan for them to travel to remote forests on inspection tours for "Protect the Earth." Billy was excited at the prospect of seeing these areas and making films.

"As soon as the baby comes and things settle down, I'll be ready to go," Billy told Larry.

I had a small office at "Protect the Earth" but I didn't go in very often, particularly of late. I decided to go one morning and Larry came in.

"Lilly, I've decided to take you up on your offer."

"Good," I said.

We discussed the price and method of payment, also changes in the administration.

"Are you ready for our attorneys to work up a contract?" I asked.

"Sure, the sooner the better."

Nathanael, Amanda and Lilly Ann were visiting us at Canaan one weekend and Nathanael mentioned that he was not happy on his job.

"It hasn't been as rewarding and fulfilling as I hoped it would be."

Immediately the thought occurred to me that maybe he would be interested in working for us. I told him of our recent partnership in "Saunders Projections."

"I'm very interested," Nathanael said. "Tell me more about it."

"I'll call Larry now," I said. "If he can come over we'll discuss it in more detail."

Larry answered and he said he could come. "Bring Teresa," I said. "She can visit with Iris and Amanda." Josie interrupted me and said, "Tell them to plan to stay for dinner."

Josie liked to cook for company and we hadn't had any dinner parties since Tony's death. She went straight to the kitchen and I knew she would come up with a gourmet meal.

Billy and Nathanael were in deep conversation; Iris and Amanda were playing with Anthony and Lilly Ann. I decided to cut some flowers and make an arrangement.

When Tony was alive I kept fresh flowers in every room in the house. He often laughed at the arrangements in his bathroom. I used masculine flowers and strong colors; no dainty frilly flowers. He particularly liked red and yellow chrysanthemums, dark colored zinnias and yellow daisies. I could almost see him now, standing in front of the mirror shaving.

"Lilly, you make me feel so special."

"That's because you are," I would say.

As I stood in our garden now and cut a large yellow zinnia and a bronze "mum" I cried out, "Oh, Tony, why did you have to leave me, I miss you so?"

But life goes on as it must just as it's supposed to do. I must be strong for my "son," Billy, and for my "grandchildren." Tony would expect me to be brave.

After dinner Nathanael, Billy, Larry and I discussed business and Larry said he would set up an appointment with Andy Zanier to meet Nathanael and go over the operation of the business.

Suddenly I felt the need to be near the water and I excused myself. I later learned from Billy that Teresa noticed I was gone and told Larry to follow me. "No, she needs to be alone," he had said.

Billy soon joined me on the beach and we cried in each other's arms. It was a release we needed. We didn't talk for awhile but when we did we spoke softly in almost a whisper. I looked out over the water I loved so much and as the waves came ashore I experienced a calmness that only comes when I'm near the water.

Billy said, "I must get back to the house. I'm sure Anthony is calling for 'daddy.'"

Larry was coming toward me as Billy left. Larry, dear, wonderful Larry. We were partners in "Protect the Earth" and now "Saunders Projections." We had endured the privations of the jungle; we had fought the insects and oh those pesky mosquitoes; and my broken foot. I had nursed him through a bad episode of a severe migraine headache. We had searched and found Sea Haven and our artist, Cecil. We shared an unusual bond that could never be broken.

He took me in his arms for the first time since the funeral. It was not a sensual moment, it was far deeper than a carnal feeling. We were both grieving the loss of a person we loved very much.

"Teresa said that I must come to you, because you needed me."

"Dear, sweet Teresa," I said. "She understands so well."

"Yes, she does," Larry said. "She's very perceptive and aware of the relationship we have. She's not jealous but compassionate and understanding—a rare quality."

"Larry, I love Teresa for her patience and her trust in both of us."

Iris was getting bigger and very weary. Anthony was extremely active as little boys are, and all of us at Canaan had a hard time keeping up with him. By noon each day Iris was exhausted so Josie and I took over in the afternoon.

But after what sometimes seems an eternity babies do come, another being on the great stage of life. What kind of world would she live in? It might be bleak unless our generation could get the message across that our land and resources must be protected.

Billy woke me at 5 a.m., "Mom, Iris is in labor. I've called the doctor and alerted the hospital. We're leaving now."

"I'll dress now and go with you."

"There's no time. Take care of Anthony. Josie is with him now. I'll call later in the morning."

Being born isn't easy, neither is dying, but day after day, month after month, and year after year the cycle continues, never ending. Now it was time to welcome a new member to our family at Canaan.

Late that afternoon at dusk Nancy Lee made her debut into the world, an eight-pound, rosy-cheeked cherub, sucking her thumb—once more the miracle of birth as life goes on uninterrupted.

Larry and Billy began making plans for their trip to the remote areas of Brazil and Peru. Two camera crews from "Saunders Projections" were assigned to the project and tons of paper work was filed with the proper authorities.

Billy was excited about the trip but was concerned about leaving Iris and the children. Iris assured him they would be fine.

"Mom, am I doing the right thing to make the trip now? Maybe I should wait another month."

"Alexander, Josie and I will take care of your family, and Nan is close by. Don't worry. You need to see the land that's in a state of erosion. Then you will have firsthand knowledge of the damage to our environment.

"Some day when Larry retires he'll want you to take his place. No one knows more than Larry how serious the conditions are that affect our health and well-being, our food supply, and even the weather."

"Oh, Mom, I don't think I'll ever be qualified to fill Larry's shoes."

"Yes, Billy, you'll be able to carry on after years of experience, more training and dedication to this very important cause. I have confidence in you."

"You're great, Mom."

Larry thought it was time to make another documentary and he was going to try to persuade Billy to do the commentary. Billy said he wasn't sure he could talk to a camera.

It was almost the one-year anniversary of Tony's death and I thought to myself, "I must do something with the sweater." The sweater was a long sleeved dark green sweater I had given Tony for his birthday. It was made of lightweight, very soft material and Tony was very fond of it.

When I came home from the hospital the day he died I went to our bedroom to weep alone. On the back of the chair next to our bed was the sweater just as he had left it. I picked it up and held it close in my arms as grief overtook me.

Every night since, I have slept with the sweater in my arms—and almost every day I have gone to his walk-in closet and gently touched each shirt, every jacket, and every sweater. The green one was special, but I realized I couldn't continue holding on. It wasn't mentally and emotionally healthy. I had to let go sometime and a year was long enough. Tony would want me to. I could almost hear him say, "Lilly, put the sweater away, turn loose and get on with your life."

"Should I burn the sweater?" I wondered. I couldn't bear that thought. If I put it in a drawer or hung it in the closet I would still be tempted to pull it out from time to time.

I decided to ask Josie. "Do you know about the green sweater?" I said.

"Yes, many times when I checked on you after you had gone to bed, I saw it in your arms."

"What should I do, burn it?"

"Oh, no, put it in a box and give it to Billy for safe keeping. Put his name on it so you won't be tempted to get it out again. I'll get a box for you."

Josie brought tissue paper and a box and left me alone to wrap it. I held the sweater one more time and brushed the soft material against my cheek. As I folded it neatly tears fell into the box. It's so hard to let go. The most difficult thing in the world is to release the hold on the past but it had to be—it was time.

Billy was in South America and Iris was on the beach with Anthony and the baby. I went to Billy's closet and placed the box on the tallest shelf, a good secret place for the time being.

Larry and Billy came back from their trip in high spirits. Billy had done half of the commentary.

"I was more comfortable than I thought," he said, "and I enjoyed it. To see the damage firsthand was quite an experience."

I could almost "see" Billy maturing and I could sense the pride Larry felt in his accomplishments. They were growing closer all the time and the strong bond between them was very evident.

One morning before leaving for work Billy knocked on my

bedroom door. "Mom," he said. The tone of his voice indicated he had something serious on his mind.

"Come in, Billy, I'm just resting," I said.

"Mom, do you think Tony would mind if I call Larry 'Dad'?"

"No, Billy, I don't think he would mind at all. Tony was once your dad but now it's Larry's turn and I know it would make Larry happy."

Billy hugged me and I felt he was going to say something else. I didn't think I could handle it at that moment.

"Don't say anything." I said. "I understand; I know what you're going to say. We'll talk another time. Go, go to work."

Tears were coming down his face; he gave me a quick kiss and was gone.

In spite of my loss, those were happy days. Watching the children grow and develop was such a pleasure. But time was racing by, as it seems to as we get older. If only the pendulum could slow down, if some hours and days could be longer, and if we could hold a particular precious moment in our hand and never let it go! But the clock of time and life will not permit it, and the pendulum goes back and forth at the same rate in its never-ending rhythm.

We can't stop the hands of time nor hold back the mighty waters rushing over the rapids—but we can take each day, one at a time, and use it productively as an example for our children and grandchildren. We can relish each precious moment to file away in our heart's memory book.

I no longer took things for granted but realized that everything and everyone had a purpose.

In the course of time Nathanael and Amanda had another baby—a boy. They named him "Nation." I was forced to ask, "Where did you get that name?"

"We live in a great, free nation—a land flowing with milk and honey in comparison with many other nations. We want him to appreciate his heritage and do what he can to protect our way of life and our environment."

"Well," I said, "he may have to explain his name to everyone he meets but maybe that will be a good thing and I understand your thinking."

When Tony had been dead a little over three years, actually three years and four months, Teresa called one afternoon.

"Hi, Lilly, what are you doing?" she asked.

"I'm reading some new material that was published recently on 'Protect the Earth.' It's encouraging and very upbeat. Billy brought it home from work."

"What's on your mind, Teresa?"

"We haven't talked in a long time, can you come over sometime soon?"

"Sure, I can come tomorrow afternoon."

"Good, Naomi will make lunch for us. She has some new recipes. How about one o'clock?"

"Fine, see you then."

Teresa and I had never had much time to be together, that is, just the two of us. She traveled throughout the States and many foreign countries. She was a known architect and very much in demand.

Teresa was one of the most talented women I had ever met. Her designs and artwork were superior. She was also beautiful and confident. Her appearance made a definite statement when she entered any room although it was not her intention.

On occasion she could be very shy and sometimes funny. I admired her greatly and I had heard she was the envy of many women, which would not impress her at all.

She was a career woman in every sense of the word and I often wondered how she could spend so much time away from home.

I never mentioned this to Larry, as it wasn't my business. Anyway, he had put his heart and soul into "Protect the Earth" and didn't seem to mind. I knew he was proud of Teresa and her accomplishments. She had received many awards and her name was a household word in architectural circles.

As I drove up the driveway at Eden the gates opened automatically. Teresa had alerted Lee, the gardener, that I would be there at one o'clock and he had opened them by remote control from the English

Garden. He waved as I went by.

Eden was beautiful—a real showplace—but quite a contrast to Canaan. Eden was elegant and formal, more European, whereas Canaan had a simple, natural style. Tony had wanted the planting to look as if it grew that way even though it didn't.

Teresa met me at the door. I thought she looked a little tired, but I knew she had recently returned from New England. She had cut back on her work and was not taking new assignments but was obligated to a client in New Hampshire to design a building to house a museum for the Historical Society.

"Lilly, I'm so glad you could come today. We don't get together enough."

"We'll have to do something about that," I said.

"Yes, indeed."

"Come, lunch is ready and then we'll talk."

I wanted to just sit and look at Teresa. Her hair was so pretty, medium brown with natural highlights of amber, almost a reddish gold. It was naturally curly too. Her deep blue eyes expressed intense emotions.

We took our coffee to the terrace and Teresa began: "Larry and I went to Chicago last week for my medical evaluation. The doctors have reason to believe the infection is returning."

"Oh, no." I didn't know what to say.

She continued, "My energy level is low again and I have a slight loss in appetite. I feel much like I did before."

"What about treatment?"

"There is a new drug now that has been about 60% effective in similar cases; however, it causes hair loss much like chemotherapy for cancer."

"I'm so sorry, Teresa, but just saying I'm sorry does not express how I really feel."

"I know, it's been a terrible blow to us but I'm willing to try the treatment even if I lose my hair."

"Will you go back to Chicago?" I asked.

"No, the Chicago doctors have referred me to Dr. Meade in Los

Angeles. He has recently treated several patients with this drug and the results have been encouraging."

"What can I do?"

"Be my friend. As you know I don't have any close friends. I've traveled so much I haven't taken time to form friendships. It's my own fault."

"I am your friend. I'll do whatever you want and need. We'll fight this together."

I left with a heavy heart but Teresa seemed relieved and relaxed.

Chapter 17

The documentary was almost completed and I was very anxious to see it. Billy was somewhat apprehensive, as he had never seen himself on a screen.

Larry planned a special preview screening for some important people in conservation. We met at "Saunders Projections" as we have a giant screen and viewing room that seats a sizable number.

I was the typical mother—nervous when her son or daughter is going to be in the spotlight. I need not have worried. Billy was a natural and looked very professional.

Teresa was scheduled for treatment three times a week. I went with her part of the time when Larry was busy. It was only a short time until her hair began to fall out.

I tried to cheer her and on days when she felt better I suggested we shop for head scarves and berets. We found a small shop on an out of the way street that had a large selection. The owner was very kind and understanding and showed us how to wrap and tie the scarves in an attractive way.

She also showed Teresa how to wear a small scarf with a beret or hat on top. It was very becoming and quite glamorous. We added long, loop earrings and she looked beautiful.

"Now, we must take pictures," I said.

"Oh no, I don't think so."

"Oh yes, we might even enter them in a fashion magazine." When Teresa looked dubious I said, "I'm not kidding."

Unfortunately, Larry and Teresa were not close to their children. She had not been at home much when they were growing up and now that they were grown they were gone.

"Where is Ruth now?" I asked.

"She's a fashion designer in Italy," answered Teresa "and is about ready to branch out on her own with a small shop. Many of her designs have been featured in prominent magazines. Originally she wanted to be a concert pianist but got involved with fashion design when she visited Italy."

"That's wonderful, and what about Jason?"

"He's studying at the London Conservatory of Music and was recently assigned assistant professor on a limited basis. He gave up on architecture."

"You and your family are so talented," I said.

"But we aren't a close family and that's what counts in the long run. I regret that I did not spend more time at home."

I couldn't disagree with that and decided it was time to change the subject.

I was constantly trying to think of things to do that would take Teresa's mind off of herself. Sometimes I would pack a picnic lunch and we would go to a park, other times the beach on a cloudy day. She was supposed to stay out of the sun as much as possible.

We both enjoyed sitting in the mall watching the people go by and wondering what their lives were like, at the same time devouring frozen yogurt.

One day she said, "Lilly, I know what you're doing, and I truly appreciate it." I pretended I didn't know what she was talking about.

More and more our friendship was reaching new levels and the bond growing stronger. This made it more painful for me in many ways but I was determined to do what I could to see her through this ordeal regardless of the outcome.

Larry was aware of the situation and mentioned it one day when we were in the office at "Saunders Projections."

"Lilly," he said, "I can't tell you how much it means to me for Teresa to have you as a friend. It has taken some of the burden from me and is a big help."

"We enjoy each other's company very much and I have the opportunity to know Teresa in a way I never thought possible," I said. "I'm sorry I can't do more."

Andy Zanier decided to retire. This meant that Larry and I had to make some adjustments in our business. We advanced Nathanael to his position and employed another man and a woman as our business was growing.

Nathanael was very appreciative and we considered him "family" but not in the same way as Billy. Nathanael was older when his father died but Billy was young and needed parents and a home.

Billy and Iris had decided to have another child to complete their family as they phrased it. Lucinda was born at midnight one very rainy, stormy night. Her birth was easier than the other two. They now had three beautiful healthy children and I had five grandchildren.

Alexander and Josie felt that they belonged to them too and I was sure they would be spoiled and unruly. They were loved so much; but you can't give children too much love if you season it with discipline and training.

Within three months Teresa was better, so much so that the injections were cut to two a week instead of three; however, her hair didn't grow back.

She didn't seem to worry about it like I thought she would. We continued to shop for attractive head coverings and I finally persuaded her to allow me to take pictures.

We didn't tell Larry, and I got Nathanael to develop them. I could hardly wait to see them and I waited outside the dark room.

"Lilly," he said, "look, these pictures are beautiful. Teresa looks like a model."

"She does indeed. I had a feeling they would be good."

"Maybe they could be submitted to medical magazines," Nathanael said, "as an encouragement to people who have lost their hair."

"We'll show them to Larry and Teresa and see what they think."

"I'll have to admit they're better than I thought," Teresa said when Nathanael and I showed them to her.

Larry said, "They're great. You're beautiful; you look like a model."

Nathanael had an idea.

"We're preparing a short subject film for the county medical association. I'll show the pictures to them and see what they think."

Larry asked me to join him and Teresa for dinner but I declined; I felt they needed time alone.

"Please come," Teresa said.

"I can't this time," I said. I made excuses and hoped it wasn't obvious. I was beginning to be aware of something not previously noticed. I didn't see the chemistry between them that should exist between married people. How could I have missed that all these years?

I knew that some people were not as demonstrative as others and certainly not in public. Tony and I had held hands all of the time and even shared a quick kiss in public occasionally. But I rationalized that we were newlyweds in comparison with Larry and Teresa. Still, I couldn't help wondering.

I didn't have to wonder many days. I had brought Teresa to the clinic for an injection and as we were leaving I said, "Where would you like to go now, any place in particular?"

"Let's go to Oceanside Park and sit on a bench near the water. We might see a few sailboats. I know you would enjoy that."

"Oh yes," I said. Oceanside was a small park not usually crowded on weekdays and was a good place for sailboats. Three were nearby and one in the distance. The thrill was always there—it was in my blood. The waves were gently rolling in whispering "Miriah," or so it seemed to me.

I waited for Teresa to speak, "I envy you, Lilly, I've envied you for years."

"Why in the world would you envy me?" I said.

"Because you have an unusual zest for life. You are passionate about everything you do. You have distributed this enthusiasm to every phase of your life, whereas I have allowed my profession to be consuming even to the detriment of my family. I neglected Larry and our children and I'm just now realizing what a mistake I've made."

I didn't know what to say. I had always felt that she should not travel so much but I couldn't say this.

"Teresa, we all make mistakes and regret them but what's done is done, it's in the past; we have to move on."

"But, Lilly, it's really bothering me. I finally got up the nerve to apologize to Larry this morning. He was so kind and sweet and said that he was sure he had made plenty of mistakes and told me not to worry about it now and to concentrate on getting well."

I put my arms around her; I didn't know what else to do. She continued, "I wrote letters to Ruth and Jason but I don't know if they will answer."

"I imagine they will. Do they know you're sick?"

"Yes, Larry called them. They both said they were sorry and would try to visit soon."

It was time to change this conversation and I said, "Come on, Teresa, let's get frozen yogurt."

She was much better by the time we got home and said, "Thanks, Lilly."

The *California Medical Beacon* was a quarterly publication featuring unusual stories about illnesses and the people connected with them.

The latest issue was on my desk at Saunders when I went in to work for awhile. I opened the cover to the first page and there was a picture of Teresa in color wearing one of the scarves we had bought. It was fantastic and I called out to Nathanael.

He entered the room smiling. "I told you we could get the pictures published. Aren't they great?"

"I can't believe it," I said.

The title read: "Teresa Mathis Battles Mysterious Infection in High Style." "Photography by Lilly Saunders."

I couldn't have been more excited if I had won the Nobel Peace Prize. "Have Larry and Teresa seen this?"

"I don't think so but they will receive several copies."

Our excitement was at fever pitch for weeks and we heard from people we had almost forgotten. Ruth called her mother from Italy. She had seen the magazine in a doctor's office and was so excited she showed it to everyone in the clinic. She also said she planned to come home for a visit in about a month.

The magazine could not have come out at a better time. It was the very thing to get Teresa out of the doldrums. They had used five of my pictures and the story that went along with them was excellent.

A side bar article read: "Lilly Saunders is well known for the environmental documentary 'Protect the Earth' made with Larry Mathis several years ago."

Local newspapers and television stations wanted to interview Teresa and she was so pleased. Larry and I cautioned her about her energy level but she was too excited to pay much attention to our advice.

The days, weeks and months that followed were good. I went to the beach early every morning to be near the water and to listen to the music of the waves. I went back in the late afternoon often followed by Anthony. His small hand in mine, we looked for seashells.

"Look, Mama, look what I found." Anthony had several names for me. Sometimes it was "Daddy's Mama,"—other times he called me "Lilly." He was growing so fast. He was losing the baby look and was becoming more and more a little boy—a precious little boy.

I looked at him and wondered what his life would be like. He was so innocent and inquisitive now. Oh, he had so much to learn, so much ahead of him. I hoped I could, someday, take him to Sea Haven and tell him about his grandmother, Laura, and also the story of my birth. Nancy Lee and Lucinda were a great pleasure too; and Iris was like a daughter.

Alexander kept the vineyard going; in fact, the vines seemed fuller than ever, and the grapes sweeter, if that's possible. Josie ran the house in a very efficient way and never appeared flustered. She was the mainstay for all of us.

Billy was appointed Executive Director of "Protect the Earth" and was Larry's right-hand man. Nathanael was practically running "Saunders Projections," and we were constantly amazed at his wisdom in making decisions.

Teresa was holding her own. She at last realized her dependency on others and was handling it in a very gracious manner. She and Larry seemed to be communicating in a way I never thought possible. They even held hands occasionally in public and I was glad.

Larry and I shared office space at Saunders as neither one of us was there for very long. One day when we were working together he said, "Let's go to lunch, I want to talk."

He started out by saying, "I'm just now realizing the serious mistakes I made in the past."

"What do you mean?" I asked.

"In a recent conversation with Teresa she said, 'Larry, why didn't you stop me? Why did you allow me to neglect you and the children?' I told her I didn't know how."

"She said, 'You should have told me I had to make a choice. You should have said, I need you, the children need you. You must decide what comes first, your job or your family. Instead you made excuses for me and defended me.'

"Lilly, I was dumb founded. She was right, but I knew her profession meant everything to her. Now, I know it was a mistake not to confront her, and I felt I had let her down and also the children. I just didn't see the whole picture at the time. Now, I have this regret that may remain with me forever."

"Larry, we all make mistakes and have regrets but we have to forgive ourselves as well as others and go on."

"That's difficult sometimes."

"Yes, it is, but just be glad you and Teresa can talk about it now."

A few months later Teresa's health began to decline again. This was discouraging as it was an indication the new medication was losing its effectiveness. We had known from the beginning that it was a possibility, but there's always hope.

Dr. Meade had been in consultation with the doctors in Chicago and the consensus was that everything had been tried but had failed. They suggested discontinuing all medication and concentrating on rest and a good diet.

At one point she tried an herbal medicine that had been recommended. It did make her feel some better but did not make a significant difference.

I felt terrible but there was nothing I could do except be with her when she wanted me. She stayed in bed more than usual but there was a calmness and peace about her, which was surprising. She liked to sit on the terrace in the late afternoon when the sun was on the other side of the house.

"I have some news," she told me. "Ruth is coming home for several months and she's bringing someone with her."

"Who is he?"

She laughed. "I thought that at first too, but she's bringing a ten-year-old Italian girl whom she has adopted."

"Oh my," I said. "What a surprise."

"Yes, it is but I'm very pleased and Larry's comment was, 'Well, this will be interesting.'"

I had never met their children. In fact, I had heard very little about them through the years.

Teresa continued, "Her name is Sabrina. She has no family. For some time she's been hanging around Ruth's shop and one morning she found her asleep at the door. After inquiries and investigations Ruth decided to keep her."

"It's a very commendable thing to do," I said. "I hope she gave the decision a lot of thought."

"Yes, I do too."

"Are you tired, Teresa? Maybe you should lie down. I'll go and let you rest."

"I believe I will lie down but I don't want you to go. Come sit by the bed."

"Lilly, I want you to make a promise."

"Certainly, if I can."

"When I'm gone, I want you to take care of Larry."

"What do you mean?"

"Promise me that you'll marry Larry."

"Teresa, I can't believe you! I can't make that kind of promise and I'm sure Larry would have something to say about it."

"I've already asked him and he said he would if you agree."

"I couldn't possibly think about anything like that now. When you told me you were very ill, it did not occur to me that you would ask me to make a promise to marry Larry."

"Lilly, I've always known you and Larry have a special relationship. I also know Larry has been faithful, and I know you would never do anything to interfere in our marriage. But I know you're so right for him, even more so than I've been."

"I won't listen to talk like this, Teresa, and I can't promise now; anyway you need to give more thought to it."

"I've thought about it for months. I know what I'm doing."

I couldn't sleep that night and for days my mind was in turmoil.

A week later Ruth arrived with Sabrina. I had not met Ruth or Jason so I was glad to get acquainted with Ruth. She was taller than Teresa and had beautiful hair like her mother. Her eyes were like Larry's and she had his magnetic smile that held me spellbound when I first met him.

Sabrina seemed small for her age. She had black hair and deep blue eyes and looked like a beautiful porcelain doll. She was shy but that was understandable. I cut back on my visits. Teresa and Ruth needed the time together without my interference and also Sabrina needed to get acquainted with her grandmother and America, a strange, new country to a little girl.

Jason came home a week later and it was a good time for Larry's family to be together and really get to know each other.

It was necessary for me to be alone to think clearly. It seemed like an eternity since we had stood in the garden at Base Camp in Africa and declared our love for one another, at the same time acknowledging the necessity of burying the feelings.

Through the years chemistry between us had surfaced occasionally, but we were always in control. In more recent years our relationship was different—we were partners in two businesses. Larry had introduced me to Tony, my dear Tony, and everything changed after that.

Those vibrant feelings of long ago had been pushed deeper and deeper into my heart and I wasn't sure they could be brought back;

much like tulip bulbs when planted too deeply don't have the strength to push through layers of earth to bloom again.

At that time I didn't think it was wise to tell Billy what was going on, but I had to talk with someone. Josie and I were very close so she was the logical one. She had always known there was a strong bond between Larry and me. I assumed Tony had told her.

Josie also knew Teresa and I had been "very close friends" in the past several months.

"I can't believe she would want you to promise to marry Larry. Why is this important to her?"

"I honestly don't know," I said.

"Lilly, you know I'm not a counselor or a therapist. My opinion would be based on life's experiences."

"I consider you to be a very wise woman," I said.

She was silent a long time, or so it seemed to me.

"Actually," she said, "your association with Larry has been through business. The attraction each of you had for the other is understandable due to the fact you have traveled together over the years—first Africa, then Sea Haven, and meetings, lectures, and conventions all across the country."

I interrupted, "That's it; do I love Larry because he is a good friend and business partner? Was our declaration of love in the garden at Base Camp a spur of the moment thing? I don't think I can promise Teresa categorically and I want to be honest with her. A number of issues would need to be resolved first."

"Tell her this," Josie said. "I think she'll understand."

"I hope so."

It had been a week since I had visited Teresa. I wanted to give her space to be with her family. I was thinking I would call when I received a call from the nurse.

"Mrs. Saunders?"

"Yes?"

"This is Mary, the nurse, Mrs. Mathis wants to know if you can come by today or tomorrow?"

"Is she worse?" I asked.

"No, she is resting comfortably."

"I can come this afternoon." I looked at my watch. It was 10:30 a.m. "What will be a good time?"

"How about between 2:30 and 3:00?"

"Fine."

I didn't know whether I would be alone with Teresa or not. If so, it was time for me to tell her that I couldn't make a definite promise but more than likely in due time I would have to make a decision.

She looked better than the week before; she was wearing one of the scarves we had bought together and was sitting up in bed. I commented on her good appearance.

"My family has been wonderful medicine for me," she said. "The children have forgiven me, Larry has forgiven me, and I have a beautiful granddaughter I never expected to have."

"Where is the family?" I asked.

"Larry took off from work today to take Ruth and Sabrina sightseeing. They were going to the zoo and a museum."

I pulled up a chair near the bed. "Before you sit down, bring me the blue box on the desk."

She took the box in her hands, held it briefly, then handed it to me.

"This is yours now."

I raised the lid; it was the blue moonbeam necklace. I gasped, "I can't take this, Teresa, no, absolutely not. Give it to Ruth."

"She doesn't want it. Both of us think it should belong to you. I told her the details of the blue stones and your connection with them. Larry and I told Ruth and Jason the Sea Haven true story."

I was visibly shaken and knew I should go. Teresa was looking tired and I didn't have anything else to say.

"Thanks for being my friend, Lilly, I don't know what I would have done the past few months without you."

"That's what friends are for," I said, "and it has been a real joy to get to really know you."

I didn't know it at the time, but that would be the last time I would see Teresa.

Chapter 18

Ruth called the next day. I wasn't at home but in my office at Saunders. Nathanael and I were going over some contracts. The call was transferred.

"I'm sorry to bother you at work," Ruth said. "I was hoping you could go to lunch with me. I assume today isn't a good day."

"I would prefer tomorrow if that's convenient."

"Fine, meet me at Andrew's at one o'clock."

Andrew's was a small elegant café patronized mostly by ladies shopping nearby. A few men would come in for lunch because of the excellent food.

Ruth was seated at a table in a quiet spot. "Thanks for coming, Lilly."

"I'm glad you called. I haven't had the opportunity to be with you alone." Looking around, I said, "This is one of my favorite places but I haven't been here in years."

"Yes, it's a charming café. I've been here once before. I thought it would be a good place to talk." She continued in a voice which was almost a whisper.

"Jason and I appreciate what you have done for Mother. She has told us the nice things you planned to make life more pleasant and bearable."

"Anyone would have done the same."

"I'm not sure about that, in fact, I doubt it. I haven't been a good daughter, Lilly. I should have called and visited more often but I always made excuses. It is very difficult to get over the bitterness I've felt for years."

"I know, Ruth, Teresa has told me that she missed Little League games, recitals, plays, the school activities—all of the things so important to children. She has agonized and worried that you and Jason would never forgive her."

"I was also angry with Dad. I thought he should have taken up for us but he always made excuses for Mother. He did his best though and attended everything he possibly could.

"Our family is reconciled now. Each one of us has admitted guilt and all is forgiven as it should be. The tension is gone and we enjoy each other, but it's sad that it was so late in coming."

"Better late than never," I said as I wiped the tears from my face. For this family it was a time of healing and renewal. Two weeks later Teresa died peacefully in her sleep, surrounded by her family.

Two weeks after the funeral I called Jason to invite him to lunch with me. I knew he was going back to London soon and I wanted to get to know him better.

"I'm glad you called, Lilly," he said as we sat down at a table in the restaurant near my office. Continuing he said, "Ruth told me of the conversation you had with her. I also want you to know that I appreciate your kindness to Mom. You've been a real friend."

"It was a privilege, Jason. Your mother was a great lady and she managed her illness in a gracious manner. She was a delight to be with on her better days. We shared joy and sorrow. I have lost a good friend and I will miss her."

"I'm leaving in two weeks. I'm giving a concert and I must practice with the orchestra. Also I'm going to play my recent composition as part of my recital work."

"How exciting! I would like to hear you play before you leave."

"And you will. I want you, Billy and Iris, Nathanael and Amanda to come to Eden one night and I'll play my composition."

"Wonderful! I'll look forward to it. Did your mother hear it?"

"Yes. I played it on a day she was feeling quite well."

I didn't ask any other questions as he was getting emotional. I knew in my heart that it must have been a very special time for mother and son.

That evening while I was on the terrace reminiscing Billy joined me.

"I want you to have something, Billy, that I put in your closet quite some time ago. It's in a box on a top shelf and I assume you haven't found it."

"No, I haven't. I can't imagine what it is."

"Let's go to your closet and I'll tell you about it."

As he took the box from the shelf, he said: "It's strange I never noticed it." When he removed the top he gasped, "It looks like Tony's sweater."

"It is," I said.

"The one you gave him for his birthday."

"Yes. Every night for twelve months following Tony's death I slept with the sweater in my arms. It's time to let go, to get on with my life. Tony would want me to."

Billy looked puzzled. "I want you to have it and wear it. I didn't want to burn it, yet I can't keep it where I see it every day."

"Won't it bother you if I wear it?" he said.

"No, I know Tony would want you to have it."

Several days later Jason invited us to Eden. Nan offered to take care of the children. Alexander and Josie were invited also. Alexander drove us in a new van he had recently purchased.

When we approached the door it suddenly opened and Sabrina was holding Larry's hand. I could tell Larry was pleased.

"This is my granddaddy," she said.

"I know," I said. "Isn't that nice?"

"Yes."

She followed Larry everywhere and wanted to sit by him while Jason played.

The composition was beautiful and Jason played like a seasoned concert pianist. Larry was obviously proud and seemed at peace.

We persuaded Jason to play other pieces and then he announced, "Sabrina is going to play with me."

He had been teaching her the past few weeks and Jason said she had a natural talent for music. She played surprisingly well. Jason apparently was a good teacher.

"Well, it seems we have two musicians in the family," said Larry.

We all agreed.

Sabrina jumped up. "Now it's time for ice cream and cake."

A child has a way of turning sorrow into joy, and hurt into healing with spontaneity. This was a time to remember, a moment to hold that passes too quickly. But Billy made a video that would bring us happiness in years to come.

Jason went back to London a week later. Ruth and Sabrina stayed another month and then....

I didn't know whether to call Larry or not. I thought maybe he needed to be alone for awhile, yet I wanted him to know I was there for him.

"What shall I do, Josie?" I asked.

"Call him and tell him that."

I waited several days.

"Hi, Larry,"

"Hi, Lilly, it's good to hear from you."

"I wasn't sure whether I should call or not."

"Of course you can call me anytime."

"When you're ready to talk or go somewhere I'm available."

"Thanks, I'll call soon."

Two weeks passed and I didn't hear from him. I wondered what was going on in his mind but I had to give him time and space.

When I least expected it, he called. I was on the terrace having a late breakfast and my second cup of coffee. Josie brought me the phone and whispered, "It's Larry."

"Hi, Larry."

"Are you busy?"

"No, I'm having a late breakfast. Actually I'm lazy today," I said.

"I would like to drive up the coast this afternoon and would like some company."

I laughed. "Are you inviting me?"

"Yes, I am."

"I would love to go."

I was trembling when I put the phone down. Josie was naturally curious.

"Well?"

"He wants to go for a drive up the coast this afternoon. He asked me to go with him."

"This is what you've been waiting for, isn't it?"

"Yes, but now I don't know what to say or how to act."

"Lilly, you've known Larry for years, you've worked together, traveled together, been through rough times together."

"This is different now. We're both free. There is no barrier. In the past we were restrained, very guarded and careful. It seems strange now and I'm scared."

"Just be natural and everything will fall into place in its own good time."

I changed dresses three times. Josie laughed at me. "You're acting like a silly school girl."

"Thanks," I said, laughing nervously.

Alexander called me from the gate to let me know that Larry had arrived. I watched him from the window. Iris and the children were playing on the lawn and he stopped to talk with them.

Josie opened the door while I tried to compose myself.

"Are you ready, Lilly?"

"I'm ready."

We drove for awhile in silence. I didn't know what to say. Finally, I gathered a bit of courage and said, "Have you heard from Jason and Ruth?"

"Yes, they called the other day. It's wonderful to have a good relationship with my children."

"And you have an added bonus, a granddaughter."

"Yes, Sabrina is great."

I noticed a road sign, "West Wind State Park, three miles." "Let's stop there," I said.

"Sure."

"I have passed the park many times but never stopped," I said.

"Neither have I."

We found a bench near the beach.

"I know you want to watch the waves," he said smiling.

My hands were trembling. I said, "Larry, I'm scared."

"I am too, Lilly."

"After all these years the situation is different now and I don't know how to handle it," I said. "I'm confused about my feelings. I do love you but I don't know what kind of love it is. So much has happened."

"You told me you loved me when we were in Africa, Lilly."

"I know but I'm not sure what kind of love I was expressing. We had been in the jungle together for weeks. When I broke my foot you took care of me. It was in a romantic setting far from home at the other end of the world. In a similar setting, I think there would be chemistry between any two people."

"But there have been other times since then when I know you had those feelings again."

"That's true. I just want to be certain the love I feel is not just friendship and the closeness we've had in business and our partnership. There have been times I wanted to hug you, hold your hand, or touch you and I've held back, afraid. Now I don't know what to do."

There was that smile again and a mischievous look. "You can hold my hand now, you can hug me and even kiss me."

I laughed. The ice had been broken and it was easier to talk.

"I want you to do something for me," I said, hesitantly. "I want you to court me."

"What?"

"Have a courtship, you know, go on dates and not talk about business. The dates would not be made at the office. You would call me at home."

"In other words you want the hearts and flowers treatment."

"I guess you could call it that. I want the dates to be separate and apart from the events of the past and the business we're in as partners."

"OK, I'll go along with this. Can we start now? How about dinner at the Rose Garden Restaurant? It's about 15 miles up the coast."

"I would love it."

The tension and apprehension were gone. We could relax. Larry now knew the reason I didn't want to give Teresa a firm promise to marry him. I wanted everything to be special, not just routine.

The Rose Garden lived up to its name. Roses were everywhere, inside and outside. Roses were in pots on a trellis and on vines. I'm sure there was every variety and color in the world. A more romantic place could not be found.

At the door a beautiful girl with a rose in her hair handed Larry a pink rose and said, "For the lady."

"To the most unique woman I've ever known," he said as he placed it in my hand. I don't think he saw the tear that fell in the center of the flower.

This was going to be more wonderful than I ever imagined.

The small dance floor on the terrace was covered with a trellis that had climbing roses hanging down. The band was setting up their instruments just as we finished dinner.

The leader approached our table and for some reason asked if it was a special occasion. We both said, "Yes."

"What kind of music do you enjoy?"

I immediately spoke up, "The big band era."

"I thought you would say that. Our band is small but we have a saxophonist which is a must with that kind of music."

"Yes, indeed," I said.

He continued, "Can I count on you to dance?"

I looked at Larry, "Of course," he said.

The first number they played was, "Let It Be Me." Larry stood, held out his hand, and in a moment I was in his arms. Was I dreaming? Was this really happening?

We didn't talk—we didn't have to. The next number was "The Very Thought of You." We drew closer and I felt comfortable laying my head on his shoulder, and I could relax for the first time in the many years we had known each other.

When we got back to Canaan I said, "It was a wonderful day and evening."

"I enjoyed it too." I knew Larry wanted to kiss me and I wanted him to kiss me too but I didn't want our courtship to move too rapidly.

I opened the door and said, "Goodnight, Larry."
   He smiled. He could read my mind.
      "Goodnight, Lilly."

Chapter 19

Jack's Art Gallery was becoming well known for attracting prominent artists. He had enlarged and remodeled the gallery and was planning a grand opening.

I was working in my office at Saunders when Jack called. "Lilly, I'm having a private reception the night before opening the gallery to the public. Cecil will be here and several artists from Europe and other countries."

"How exciting!" I said.

"I would like for you and Larry to assist me as hosts. Both of you are known for your documentary on 'Protect the Earth' and your subsequent lectures."

"We would be honored. I'm sure Larry would agree."

"I'm going to call Larry now," Jack said, "and I'll get back to you later on the details. I'm not sure of the date yet but probably two or three weeks."

Larry called later, "You've talked with Jack?"

"Yes, what do you think?"

"I believe it's a good way to advertise his gallery and introduce these artists to the community. It will be an honor to have a part in it."

"Yes," I said.

"By the way, Lilly, will this event be considered a courtship date?"

"You're teasing me, Larry, and making fun of me; you know it won't be a date. Just wait until I see you."

"I wanted to know if it would be an occasion for me to send you flowers."

"You can always send me flowers. Goodbye, Larry."

I loved Larry's voice—it was so strong yet not too loud—the

voice of a man with confidence and self-esteem at the same time, not egotistical but compassionate and caring, always thinking of others. This was the reason I had been drawn to him many years ago.

Larry was never dull or boring. At times he came up with priceless one-liners but always a man on a mission—a mission to acquaint the world with the problems of our environment.

Some days I wondered why I was hesitant. Why didn't I tell Larry I was ready to marry him? What was I waiting for? For some unknown reason I felt I would know the perfect time, but is there ever a perfect time for anything? We can strive for perfection but never quite achieve it. That's the way life is.

Nathanael interrupted my thoughts with a business matter jarring me back into the real world. Then the next thing that came to mind was, "I need a new dress."

That night I decided to call Cecil. I hadn't talked with him in a long time. Miriam answered the phone. She said Cecil was busy in the studio.

"That's all right. I'll talk with you. I'm excited about the reception. Jack called this morning."

"Yes, we're excited too. Larry has invited us to stay at Eden. It will be nice to see everyone again and also to meet artists from different parts of the world. Cecil is finishing a painting he has been working on a long time that he wants to exhibit. It's a portrait of Joseph and me."

"I can hardly wait to see it," I said.

"I'm very pleased but it's a strange feeling to see myself on canvas as my husband sees me. Joseph loves it."

I asked Iris to go shopping with me the next week.

"I probably should get a new dress too," she said. "I've increased one dress size since the birth of the children."

We had heard of a new shop recently opened.

"Let's try it," I said.

Nan was more than willing to keep the children. Iris found a dress almost immediately—a shade of blue that matched her eyes and looked beautiful with her dark hair.

It took me longer. After trying on several I finally found the perfect one. It was mauve chiffon with delicate pink flowers in the design. Everyone in the shop gathered around when I came out wearing it and all agreed it was made for me.

On the way home Iris said, "Larry will flip when he sees you in this dress."

"Well, I sure hope so," I said with a laugh.

Larry and I enjoyed the same things—the theater, concerts, gardens, special exhibits, basketball and golf. Tony had been teaching me to play when he got sick.

"It's time you got back on the greens," Larry said and I agreed.

"You'll have to be patient with me, Larry."

"Of course."

He was taking our courtship very seriously and was always planning new things to do.

"Let's go to the Band Shell Park on a picnic."

"When?"

"Tomorrow, I'll bring the food."

The park was about twenty miles away and at certain times had band music.

Larry was a good cook, specializing in gourmet foods. His salads were delicious and I was anxious to see what was in the basket. It was a better meal than we would have in most restaurants. The dessert was out of this world—pound cake with almond sauce, topped with strawberries and whipped cream.

He had brought a quilt for us on which to spread the lunch. After we ate Larry stretched out on the quilt. I was sitting up looking at it and he said, "My grandmother made it. It is called patchwork. She gave it to me when I finished high school."

I examined the quilt and looked at him. After all these years I didn't know much about his forebears.

"What about your grandmother?" I said.

"She died the year I finished college. She was a wonderful woman and I enjoyed her company. Many of my cooking secrets came from her."

Larry was getting grayer and had more lines in his face. Men have lines; women have wrinkles. Suddenly I felt older than usual.

I studied his face—so strong, so beautiful, not handsome or pretty; but his good character was reflected in his eyes showing compassion, love, and caring. He pulled me to him and I lay in his arms, my head on his shoulder; he placed my hand over his heart.

For the first time, I knew without a doubt I loved him and was in love with him, but I didn't say anything. We were silent going home but when we reached Canaan he said, "Are you all right?"

"Yes."

At the door I hesitated. He took me in his arms and lifted my face toward him; this time I cooperated as he kissed me. Finally, I reluctantly pulled away as the situation was getting too steamy.

"Goodnight, Larry."

"Goodnight, Lilly."

Cecil and Miriam arrived the day before the reception and Larry prepared dinner that evening with a little help from Naomi. They had set up the table on the terrace overlooking the Japanese garden. For a brief moment, as the four of us enjoyed the meal, my mind drifted back to Teresa. She loved this garden so much, but I think she would be pleased to know I had made a decision.

After dinner Miriam wanted me to look at the dress she planned to wear for the reception. It was pink silk, a fitted long dress with cap sleeves and mandarin collar.

"Oh, Miriam, it's beautiful."

"Cecil took me to Seattle. I tried on three but he liked this one."

"An excellent choice. I'm anxious to see you in it."

"I'm curious, Lilly. What's going on with you and Larry?"

I'm sure I blushed. "We're courting."

"You're what?"

I explained the situation and she said, "That's great and how are things progressing?"

"Very well, I'll keep you and Cecil informed."

Jack was having a light buffet for the visiting artists and their spouses before the reception. Peter had agreed to drive them to the

Gallery in the limousine.

Josie helped me get dressed. I was very nervous and excited.

"Lilly, everyone is going to be looking at you."

"No, Josie, they're going to be looking at Miriam. Her dress is gorgeous and she's young and beautiful."

"But you're natural and beautiful."

"Josie, you're so good for me. I could never get along without you."

Larry came to the door with a corsage—a large pale pink orchid, perfect with my dress.

Josie opened the door and when I entered the room Larry stopped and stared.

"Say something, Larry," I said.

"I have never seen you look more beautiful."

He was visibly shaken and told Josie she should pin the orchid on my shoulder. I didn't want to ruin my lipstick but I had to kiss him. After all, lipstick can be replaced.

Billy, Iris, Nathanael and Amanda were coming later as they wouldn't stay long. Since Larry and I were hosts we would be there all evening.

Jack had told us to come about fifteen minutes before the other guests so we could meet the artists. It was so exciting to be in the company of world famous artists and to see their work.

I wanted to see Cecil's portrait of Miriam and Joseph. Larry and I agreed it was superior.

It was a truly wonderful evening, but by midnight I was exhausted and glad when all the guests were gone and we could go home. For some reason the affair had been very draining.

I told Larry I was going to sleep the next day and would call him later. I didn't call until five in the afternoon.

"That's all right," he said, "Cecil, Miriam and I slept until three this afternoon and I took them to the airport."

"Larry, I want to be alone for a couple of days. Do you mind?"

"No, Lilly, do what you have to do."

Two nights later I called.

"I want to take you out to dinner."

"You want to take me out?"

"Yes, Larry, I'm asking you for a date."

"You're full of surprises. What do you have in mind?"

"Tomorrow night. I'll pick you up."

"Where are we going?"

"It's a surprise. I'll pick you up at seven—dinner and dancing. I'm going to drive."

"Can you give me a hint?"

"No," I said with a laugh.

"OK, see you at seven."

Lee was at the gate when I got to Eden. "Don't tell Larry I'm here, I want to go to the door."

Larry liked Gerbera daisies, especially a shade of pinkish orange. They were hard to find sometimes but I had been lucky that day. When he opened the door I handed him five Gerbera mixed with blue lace, a type of wild flower.

Oh there was that smile again.

"You brought me flowers? If I didn't know better I'd say you were courting me."

"You're right. Ready to go?"

"Ready."

When we had gone about ten miles Larry asked, "How much farther?"

"Oh no, you're trying to trick me. You'll know soon enough."

We were approaching another five-mile marker and I knew he would guess, but he didn't say anything.

We turned off the main road onto a side road and into the parking lot.

"The Rose Garden," he said, "you're taking me to the Rose Garden. We had our first date here."

"Yes, we did."

I had made a reservation and we were ushered to a private table adjoining the rose-covered terrace.

"Shall we dance while we wait for our dinner?" I said. The

bandleader smiled and winked as they started playing the same songs that were played the first time. I had made the arrangements.

"This is a set-up," Larry said.

"Don't talk, just dance."

This time there was no uncertainty. I was confident of my feelings and what I planned to do. We were dancing close, cheek to cheek; I felt his breath on my hair and his lips on my face—and then on my lips.

It was the height, depth and width of true love, a rare and beautiful thing, which everyone doesn't find. We were so fortunate and Teresa had been very wise. She knew we should be together.

When dinner was over I walked out on the terrace. Larry followed. No one else was there. I think the manager was escorting people to the other end of the restaurant so we could be alone.

"Lilly, you're the most romantic woman I've ever known."

"That's me. Sometimes I think too much so."

"No," Larry said, "I like it. You make everything special and I feel special."

"You are. I've loved you for a long time and I know now I'm in love with you. Will you marry me, Larry?"

He was stunned; I had caught him off guard. "You're proposing to me? I can't believe it."

"Well, don't keep me waiting."

"Yes, I'll marry you."

The kiss that sealed our commitment was the kind that every woman should experience at a time like this.

A path through the garden led to a small beach on the water. We followed it and found a bench. We shared another kiss and sat quietly for a few minutes.

Larry spoke first. "When and where do you want to get married?"

"How about as soon as we can make the arrangements?"

"Fine, and did you have a place in mind?"

"Some small church not connected with any other event in our lives," I said.

"The church we have been attending lately is nice."

"Yes, it is. We can check with the minister. Let's go and tell everyone at Canaan."

Josie was excited and Billy said, "Well, it's about time, Mom, I'm so pleased."

Larry asked, "Do you think we can get a wedding together in two weeks?"

"I don't see why not," Josie said.

The next day Larry and I made an appointment with the minister at the Shady Grove Church. We had met Dr. Edmundston on several occasions but he didn't know anything about us.

Larry thought he should know our story beginning with our first meeting in my office at the university up to the present time. Larry unfolded the events of our lives that had molded us into the two people we were now.

"Amazing," said Dr. Edmundston. "It sounds almost like fiction—your unusual birth, Lilly, and the events that followed."

It was decided that the wedding would take place in two weeks at four o'clock in the afternoon. We wanted it small and simple, only family and a few close friends.

Larry had called Jason and Ruth but they would not be able to come. We promised we would visit them soon.

Billy and Iris wanted to have dinner afterwards at Canaan. Josie and Naomi would prepare the food. We could use the large dining room that was seldom used. Tony had preferred small dinner parties.

There was very little shopping to do as I already had my dress. Josie persuaded me to go with her to a bridal shop. She wanted me to have some exotic lingerie.

Chapter 20

A new lodge had recently opened in the mountains north of the city about 25 miles away. It had a number of rooms, a restaurant and recreational facilities, also several individual cabins for more privacy. The brochure advertised the Green Mountain Lodge as the perfect honeymoon getaway. We made a reservation for a two weeks stay.

The big question—where were we going to live?

We didn't want to live at either Canaan or Eden. We needed to make a complete new beginning.

"Do you want to build a house?" Larry asked.

"No, I don't want to go through all the problems and work involved in building. Maybe we can find a house already built. I wouldn't mind remodeling a house if we liked the basic plan and location."

Larry owned an apartment complex and several condos. "Surely, one of these is vacant and we could live in one while we look for a house."

We made an appointment with Leona Moreland, a prime property agent, to discuss what kind of house we would like.

"It may be impossible," I said, "but I would like a place near the water so I can have a sailboat."

And now on a late summer afternoon, on a day similar to the day Larry and I looked for Sea Haven almost twenty years ago, I became Larry's wife. So much had happened during the intervening years; many people had come into our lives, even becoming part of our families. I looked at Billy and Nathanael who had brought us so much joy—their precious children now considered our grandchildren.

Larry and I had both lost spouses we loved but the living must carry on, perhaps experiencing a new and deeper meaning of love.

What is that old saying, "Grow old along with me, the best is yet to be." Larry and I could look forward to a life together filled with hope, excitement and love that could never be expressed in words.

The time had come; our time was at hand; Dr. Edmundston was standing in front of us, Bible in hand; Larry was looking at me and smiling—the smile that had captured my heart long ago. Amanda was playing the violin. Billy, Iris, Nathanael and the children were there. The silence was deafening; an air of anticipation permeated the small building. Even Joshua, holding Joseph on his lap, was quiet. Cecil and Miriam's presence was an additional joy for us, as well as that of Jack from the art gallery, who had been an important part of our lives. Josie, Alexander, Peter, Naomi and Lee completed the audience.

Larry and I had purposely made our vows short. We had already made commitments privately, intimate things we didn't want to share.

Since Dr. Edmundston knew our story his remarks were appropriate and meaningful. When he announced we were husband and wife Anthony spoke up from his seat and said, "Amen."

Everyone laughed. Little children have an innocent way of making memorable occasions more so.

We persuaded Dr. Edmundston and his wife to join us for dinner. Billy said, "Alexander and Josie want you to see their vineyard and vegetable garden."

Peter and Naomi, with Lee's help, had decorated Canaan with flowers from the gardens at Eden. It looked like a veritable botanical garden. Two cameramen from Saunders came to make a video and also still photographs. Cecil had a sketch pad, and he made an outline of the terrace and fountain to later put on canvas.

Just as we prepared to sit down for dinner the doorbell rang. Larry said, "I'll get it." In walked the members of the five-piece band from the Rose Garden Restaurant.

Larry had made arrangements for them to come without my knowledge.

"Larry," I said, "I can't believe you did this."

"Our first date was at the Rose Garden and you proposed to me there. We pledged our love listening to their music."

The bandleader, Evis, spoke up, "We're honored to be here and to be a part of your marriage celebration."

I was completely overwhelmed and wished I could go in a room to myself and cry. Larry noticed that I was emotional and he asked the band to play; then he swept me into his arms and we danced in a small area Josie had cleared away. The song was, "There Will Never Be Another You."

The table looked like a banquet. Billy was master of ceremonies and wanted everyone to make a short speech. Billy spoke first. "This wonderful woman, Lilly, my mom, together with Tony and Larry, have made it possible for me to have a life I would not have had otherwise."

Nathanael expressed his appreciation for what we had done for him.

Jack told how he had met Larry and me when we came to his gallery looking for a mysterious artist.

Cecil told of our visit to Sea Haven that had resulted in a long-term friendship, and Joshua in his faltering yet beautiful manner recounted the story of the "water baby."

Larry was an excellent speaker. For years he had held people spellbound with his lectures on conservation and "Protect the Earth." This occasion was no exception as he addressed each one personally. Turning to me, he said, "Lilly, thank you for loving me, for becoming my wife, my companion, my lover and the joy of my life."

I was last and there was nothing left for me to say. With tears flowing freely down my face I managed to say, "I love all of you, my cup truly overflows, spilling into the saucer."

A limousine arrived to drive us to the Green Mountain Lodge (this was part of the package). As we ran down the walkway the children threw rose petals and scattered them on the path. The chauffeur said it was an hour and ten minutes drive so I relaxed in Larry's arms with my head on his shoulder. We didn't talk. Now and then he leaned over to give me a reassuring kiss.

It was still hard to believe that he was now my husband. For almost twenty years we had been associated in many other ways—

the documentary, co-lecturers, partners in business and friends. We had numerous interests in common.

But it was a different story now. This man sitting so close that I could feel his heart beat and his breath on my hair and face was to be my companion, my protector and my lover. We had entered that most intimate and magical relationship—the union of two people who love each other so deeply, so passionately, that they will become one. It was a little frightening but exciting.

In the past I had allowed myself for a few brief moments to imagine a time like this, never dreaming it could ever come true.

"Here we are, welcome to Green Mountain Lodge."

I hadn't noticed when we left the interstate and turned onto a rural road. The lodge was built into the side of a mountain. A lake was in front; several log cabins surrounded the lake, well-spaced, providing privacy.

Our cabin had a front porch with rocking chairs. Inside the decor was rustic but not primitive except there was no television and no telephone. A combination radio, tape and CD player was on a table next to the fireplace. A large sofa and several chairs gave the room an air of comfort and warmth.

A small kitchen was equipped with a well-stocked refrigerator. A large basket of fruit was on the table. The bedroom was big and furnished luxuriously. A fresh-flower arrangement of mammoth proportions was the centerpiece of the room. It was very romantic. We couldn't have selected a more perfect honeymoon hideaway.

Larry spoke first. "This is our first home, Lilly, our home for two weeks. Do you like it?"

"I love it."

And so it was here in this remote setting, away from the outside world, surrounded by the beauties of nature, even a creek just outside our bedroom window with water flowing over the rocks in musical rhythm, that Larry and I came to know each other in the biblical sense. Words cannot describe, nor should they be used, to convey the beauty, powerfulness, passion and love that blended our lives into one.

For two weeks we stayed mainly to ourselves going to the Lodge in the evening for dinner and dancing. Most of the couples there seemed to have the same need for privacy, shutting out the world and its problems.

We followed a wild flower trail, sat on a riverbank and discovered a rainbow in the waterfall. Many evenings we sat on the porch and watched as the sun set and appeared to melt into the horizon.

I was certain I was the happiest, most fortunate woman in the world. Sometimes a person anticipates and hopes for a special happening, not knowing if it will occur; then when it does come about the excitement diminishes to a degree.

This was not true in my case. Loving Larry and being loved by him exceeded my expectations far beyond what I had ever hoped or dreamed. My thoughts went back to Teresa when she told me shortly before her death, "Lilly, I didn't fully appreciate what I had. Now I know, but it's too late."

The two weeks were over. It was time to go home and I was anxious to start our lives in the real world. Larry called Billy from the Lodge and told him we were coming home.

"Your apartment is ready," Billy told Larry, "and I think your real estate agent has some news for you."

As soon as we got to the apartment Larry called Leona.

"I've found a house you may be interested in," she said. "The property has been in dispute for over a year but the suit has been settled and is for sale. It needs quite a bit of repair but has possibilities."

"When can we see it?"

"I'm busy today but I will bring photographs to you and information on the property. I can take you to see it tomorrow."

The house was on the channel, on slightly elevated land with a beautiful beach. It looked majestic as if it were overseeing its surroundings.

"I love it!" I said.

"Don't get too excited, photographs can be deceiving. It does appear to have charm and an inviting appearance."

I could hardly wait to see the house and the surrounding area. Leona picked us up the next morning. Twenty-five miles from the city limits we left the interstate and turned onto a rural road.

"The house is six miles from here," Leona said. We passed several well-kept and beautiful houses.

I saw the water and the beach first and then on the right side of the road the house came into view. No one had lived in it for over a year and it was in need of repair.

"It has character and personality," I said, "but it needs extensive renovation. What do you think, Larry?"

"I agree. The question is, do we want to spend the amount of time it would take to make it into what we want?"

We decided to go home and think about it. Also we wanted to tell Billy and the others.

Larry called David, an architect who had worked with Teresa. He said he would be glad to look at the house and determine what could be done. Billy wanted to look at the house also.

Two weeks later David presented us with an architectural design we both liked. He said, "It will take at least ten to twelve months to complete, that is if we're lucky with materials and labor."

"What do you think, Lilly, are you willing to wait?" Larry asked.

"Yes, I think it's what we've dreamed of. Let's go for it."

Chapter 21

Larry and I decided to visit Jason in London. Billy said he would oversee the renovation, and David assured us he would be on hand also.

It was wonderful to see Jason again. We met his friend, Maria, who was a violinist. They appeared to be in love.

"Is this serious?" Larry asked.

"Yes, it is," Jason answered, grinning broadly. "We're planning to be married in four weeks and we're hoping you can be persuaded to stay for the wedding."

Larry explained that we were renovating a house and didn't want to be gone too long.

I interrupted, "But we had planned to visit Ruth and Sabrina in Naples. Larry, do you think we could visit them and come back to London for the wedding?"

We put in a call to Billy. Iris answered the phone, "Billy's at your house."

"How are things going?" Larry asked.

"Fine, all of the materials came in on time and everything is on schedule. There haven't been any problems so far. I think you could carry on with your plans without worry."

"How are the children?"

"Good, they're very excited about your house. Billy says he's going to get a sailboat to keep there after you move in. Anthony is driving us crazy to know how long it will be."

"Time goes slowly for children, especially when they are looking forward to something."

Several days later we flew to Naples. Ruth and Sabrina were at the airport.

"Sabrina, you have grown so much," I said.

She seemed pleased as she hugged me. Young girls always want to grow up, anxious to become women, but all too soon there will be times when they wish to be young again.

Ruth's condominium was on the third floor overlooking the sea. The view was breathtaking. Watching the waves come ashore caused my heart to beat a little faster.

"I may never want to leave, Ruth," I said.

"You know why I love it so."

"Yes."

"Let me show you your bedroom. I think you and Dad will like it. Some nights you can raise the windows and hear the waves and in the mornings you can see the sunrise over the sea."

Sabrina was taking ballet and piano lessons. Jason had encouraged her with the music and was able to fly down occasionally to teach her special techniques.

We were amazed at her ability. Too, she reminded us of Jason with body language similar to his. While we were there Sabrina had a ballet recital and again she surprised us.

I said to Ruth privately, "Sabrina is a very intelligent girl and you are fortunate to have her and she's lucky to have you."

The days that followed were like another honeymoon. Sabrina and Ruth were gone most days. Larry and I had the condo to ourselves. The bedroom was large, luxuriously furnished with windows across one entire wall looking out on the sea. I'm sure there wasn't another place on earth as romantic.

Time doesn't stand still for a single moment and all too soon it was time to go back to London. After all we had a wedding to attend. Ruth and Sabrina were able to get on the same flight with Larry and me.

The wedding took place in the garden of the Conservatory of Fine Arts. Some of Jason's and Maria's musician friends provided beautiful music—love songs played on the harp and violin. After the reception Jason took us to the airport. Ruth and Sabrina left on an earlier flight to Naples.

"Dad, you'll never know what it has meant to me for you and Lilly to have been here for my wedding." All of us were a little teary. Jason promised that he and Maria would visit us when we moved into our new house.

When we were settled on the plane I said, "It's been a great trip, hasn't it?"

"Yes, it has, I'm glad we came."

Billy met us at the airport. "Hi you two, I've missed you."

Dear Billy, sometimes when I looked at him I could see the young boy, worried and afraid when his mother was so sick. Now, he was a grown man, efficient in business, a loving family man and a son to me. Oh, Laura, I wish you could see him—you would be so proud.

We had been gone over a month but it seemed much longer. I could hardly wait to see our house.

Larry was evidently thinking the same thing. "How's the house coming?" he asked.

"Great! Actually, they're ahead of schedule now but still a long way to go. I'm pleased with it, and I think you will be too."

I needed to rest a few days as I was wiped out from jet lag. Larry called David to get a report on the renovation.

"Wait a few days," he said. "Some walls are going up and we'll be able to visualize better."

Meanwhile Larry was thinking about Eden.

"I don't want to sell it. I would like to come up with a plan to preserve it in some way that would benefit others. Do you have an idea, Lilly?"

"Yes, I've been giving it some thought. The gardens at Eden are so beautiful and unique they should be opened to the public, at least part of the time; and maybe we could provide classes in landscaping and gardening. We might even set up a scholarship fund for students in these and related subjects."

"Lilly, your wheels have been spinning. I like it, and we could call it The Teresa Mathis Scholarship Fund and the gardens could be dedicated in her memory."

"Exactly. This is exciting; I'm ready to get started. With a few changes and remodeling the house could be used for classrooms."

Larry's mind was in high gear now.

"We could also have classes on conservation and the environment."

"How about a section on architecture?" I suggested. "We could have displays of Teresa's buildings on the walls."

"Perfect. By taking down a few walls and combining rooms there would be plenty of space."

We decided that the next move should be to discuss these plans with Lee, Peter and Naomi. They liked the ideas and were very enthusiastic.

Lee took so much pride in the gardens and said, "It will be a real pleasure to show the gardens to the public."

Naomi said, "Eden will come alive again and will be a benefit to the community."

It was decided that Peter would continue to maintain the property outside and inside. Naomi would be the official hostess.

Larry made another call to David, the architect, explaining our plans. He was excited too and said he would like to bring one of his associates with him.

Our house was progressing to the point that Larry and I had to make decisions on various phases of the work. Some suggestions we had made turned out not to be feasible so alternative plans had to be implemented. Overall, we were pleased with the results.

When Larry and I married and moved into the condo, the only furniture he took from Eden was his desk, chair, and lamp from his study. The condo was furnished but we found a place for the desk. It was temporary anyway until we could move into our house.

The next decision was what to do with the furniture at Eden. Larry called Jason and Ruth and told them of our plans for Eden. We asked them to come and select the things they wanted.

"It would be good if both of you could be here at the same time to choose what each of you would like to have," Larry told them.

They would have to work it out and call us later.

We made an appointment with David and Jeanine to meet us at

Eden. Jeanine was David's associate and she had also worked with Teresa. She was very anxious to work on the project.

At first I was somewhat worried that Peter and Naomi might not approve of Eden being converted to a public building. After all it had been their home for a long time. Jason and Ruth had grown up under their watchful eye because their mother was gone so much.

But surprisingly they were enthusiastic and well aware that Larry could not keep Eden as a home. They would continue to be a major part of an important project, and still have their house on the grounds.

Lee lived on the property also in a small gardener's cottage. We decided to enlarge it and build a connecting green house.

Lee was very excited. He said, "Now I can develop new specimens of plants and flowers."

"Yes," Larry said. "It will be all yours to do whatever you want."

Jeanine had several good ideas that she had thought of, and Larry and I were more than willing to incorporate them into the overall plan.

Jason arrived a week later. Maria decided not to come but wanted to wait for the grand opening.

Officials with the conservation department and the "Protect the Earth" project were planning a banquet to honor the people who had made contributions of time or money to advance awareness of environmental problems and disasters.

Larry asked me what I was going to wear. This was rather unusual, I thought.

"I don't know yet. We've been so busy with decisions about our house and making plans for Eden that I haven't really thought about it. Why do you ask?"

He hesitated. "I want you to wear the blue moonbeam necklace. You haven't worn it yet, have you?"

"No."

"Teresa gave it to you to wear and enjoy. I would like for you to wear it to the banquet with the earrings."

"I guess it is time. I was afraid it would upset you. Also it will be strange for me."

"Lilly, we have to let go of many things in the past, but we can still cherish the memories."

Jason was pleased with our plans for Eden.

"Dad," he said to Larry, "I would like to have the furniture in your bedroom if it's all right."

"Of course, and when Ruth comes you can divide some of the other things."

There was enough china, silver and crystal for them to share, but Ruth and Jason were in agreement that the crystal should be left and perhaps displayed in a glass case.

Ruth wanted Teresa's bedroom furniture, plus one small table and lamp. Both she and Jason had excellent suggestions about rearranging the living room as a conference area and place for the host and hostess desk.

Jason and Ruth could only stay a few days but they wanted to see the plans David and Jeanine had drawn up. It was decided that the two bedrooms, den and library would be made into classrooms. The dining room was to remain as it was for the time being.

They also wanted to see our house, so Larry and I drove them out the day before they left.

"Sometimes," Jason said, "I wish I was back in the States. There's so much going on in the family. I would like the opportunity to get to know Billy and his family better, also Nathanael and his family."

Ruth agreed.

"When my business is more stable Sabrina and I may be in a position to visit for several months at a time."

They liked the house and the location and promised to come back when it was completed, which we hoped would coincide with the public opening of Eden.

Several days later I said to Larry, "We must decide what we want to call Eden. It must have an official name for advertising and other purposes."

We wanted to keep it simple but at the same time informative. After discarding several sheets of paper we came up with this: "The Teresa Mathis Memorial Gardens and Eden Institute." The brochure would list the courses—landscaping and gardening, conservation and environmental studies, as well as advanced architecture. It was quite an ambitious undertaking but we felt we could do it with lots of help and good instructors. We had our work cut out.

Lee was so excited and enthusiastic, we had to calm him down at times. Peter and Naomi talked about it constantly. Larry and I laughed about their exuberance. With so much exhilaration there was no way it could fail.

Billy and Nathanael agreed to help with advertising. Nathanael had a great idea for the format of the brochure. But first we had to get instructors for the different courses.

Lee had a cousin who had just obtained his degree in landscaping. He thought he could get him to help with classes. Lee preferred to lecture during a tour of the gardens and people could make notes.

David had a friend who had recently retired, but he thought he might be willing to teach a few classes on architecture. David and Jeanine said they would be willing to fill in from time to time.

Conservation was a different matter. Offhand, Larry said he couldn't think of anyone who could teach in that area.

"What about you, Larry?" I asked.

"I don't consider myself a teacher," he said. "I'm more of a lecturer."

"Maybe we shouldn't start all of the classes at the same time," I said, "but add them gradually."

"We have our house to work on, too," Larry said. "We don't want to overextend ourselves."

There were many legal matters to take care of before opening the Institute, which always takes a long time. We didn't want to rush and there were so many facets of this undertaking that we wanted everything as perfect as possible.

Larry and I had neglected our house when we became so enthused about the conversion of Eden, so now it was time to concentrate on the house. The major change we had made was to change the front entrance to face inland, the side of the house to face the road, and the back toward the water, overlooking the channel.

Several walls had been removed to make the house appear larger and more open. We wanted to bring the outdoors inside as much as possible. I had not seen the house in ten days; Larry had been checking on it while I was tied up with paper work. I was amazed. "I can't believe it," I said. "It looks just as I had imagined, even better."

"Wait until you see the terrace," Larry said.

The living room and dining room had been combined into one very large room that would be divided by furniture placement. Sliding glass doors opened onto a lattice-covered terrace with a perfect view of the channel. We could hear and see the waves. A few sailboats were anchored in the harbor and two schooners were returning from taking supplies to a nearby island.

"It reminds me of Sea Haven," I said. "It's a dream come true."

Larry smiled—that same beautiful smile that had captivated me from the beginning. He held me close. "I'm so glad you're pleased."

At times it was still difficult for me to realize that Larry and I were married. I never imagined years ago when I broke my foot in the jungle, and Larry carried me in his arms, that someday we would belong to each other.

I remembered the throbbing pain in my foot and my pounding heart as he carried me and I felt his breath on my face and hair.

"Lilly, what are you thinking about? You seem to be miles away."

"I was thinking about those days in the jungle." I was sure I was blushing.

"I recall them once in awhile too."

I didn't want to talk any longer. I wanted to get lost in his arms, so soft, so secure, so loved.

Chapter 22

We moved into our house six weeks later, arranging and rearranging our furniture several times. Billy and Iris helped and finally we agreed on the placement of everything.

Billy and his family visited often; the children loved it. One day Billy was on the terrace alone looking out toward the water.

"Billy, does this place remind you of Sea Haven?"

"Yes, it does, I love it."

"I do too."

One day when we had been in our house about two months, Larry said, "I have a surprise for you but I need to blindfold you and we're going down to the harbor."

"Oh my, I can't imagine what you're up to."

Sometimes we would walk to the harbor but Larry said it would be better to drive this time. When we stopped he helped me out of the car and led me by the hand to the water's edge. I knew we were near the water; I could always sense it and I also heard waves in their ceaseless journey as they came ashore.

"I'm going to remove the blindfold now."

I never expected what I saw. It was the most beautiful sailboat I'd ever seen, and...on the side was painted the words, "The Water Baby." The gamut of emotions took over. I cried, I laughed, and I screamed.

"This is unbelievable. I never would have expected this. Oh Larry, Larry, you know me all too well."

"Billy is going to teach us how to operate the boat. Here he comes now."

He jumped out of the car and grabbed me. "Mom, what do you think?"

"I'm speechless. Did you know about this?"

"Yes, I knew whom to contact. Dad and I wanted you to have the finest sailboat in the world. I'm getting one similar to this one. I want my children to know the joy and exhilaration of sailing."

"For me," I said, "there's nothing like floating along with the breeze silent except for the sound of the water, as the boat is controlled to a certain degree by the wind in the sails."

"Lilly, would you like to have a christening party to officially name 'The Water Baby?'"

"Oh yes, Larry, I'd love it. Billy, when will your boat be here? You could christen yours at the same time."

"I'll check on it."

The christening turned out to be quite an event. Nathanael suggested we include a house blessing for our new home.

Josie and Naomi prepared food. Lee brought flowers from Eden. There had been no time yet to do landscaping and planting. Lee said he would prepare a garden as soon as he finished the gardens at Eden.

We invited Dr. Edmundston and his wife, and Jack, David and Jeanine. Larry invited the people from his office and Nathanael arranged for one of his camera crews to make a video. Three other families lived on the road leading to the harbor and we included them.

All of us gathered at the harbor. Larry spoke, "We're here to christen two sailboats. One belongs to my wife and the other to our son, Billy. Some of you don't know the story of Sea Haven and the water baby. Lilly and Billy will be glad to tell you sometime."

Larry handed me a bottle of champagne and I nervously held it by the neck.

"I christen you 'The Water Baby.'" He then gave the other bottle to Billy.

"I christen you 'Sea Haven II.'"

The children went crazy. We finally calmed them down enough to go to the house. Dr. Edmundston had prepared a short speech. Then it was time to enjoy the delicious food. Naomi and Josie had outdone themselves.

Larry held my hand and kissed me tenderly as tears rolled unashamedly down my face. Once again my cup was overflowing and spilling into the saucer.

Six weeks later we were ready to have the grand opening of the Garden and Institute. Ruth and Sabrina came a week early and we asked them to stay with us. I knew Sabrina would like the sailboat and she did, wanting to go out as soon as they arrived.

Late one afternoon Larry said, "Sabrina, are you ready to go sailing?"

"Yes," she said, dancing all over the place.

The weather was perfect for sailing and as I helped Larry raise the sails, once again a flood of emotion carried me back to the time Laura and Billy took Larry and me sailing at Sea Haven.

Now this precious little girl was discovering the joy and wonder of sailing that had held me captive for years.

Chapter 23

After much deliberation the decision was made to limit the grand opening at Eden to city officials, people in the areas of landscaping, gardening, conservation, architecture and civic clubs, plus close friends.

Jason and Maria arrived two days early and Cecil, Miriam, Joseph and Joshua came the day before.

Larry had not mentioned the blue moonbeam necklace again and I had not worn it.

"Larry, if you want me to I'll wear the necklace with my earrings to the grand opening."

He was visibly moved. "I would like that, Lilly."

I had a dress that matched the necklace and earrings but I wanted a new one. I asked Ruth to go shopping with me.

"I'd love to, Lilly. I may get a new dress also."

I wanted to form a bond with Jason and Ruth but at the same time not leave the impression I was trying to take the place of their mother. I was pleased how well they both had responded. Larry had noticed the affection we manifested to one another and told me how much he appreciated it.

"They're easy to love, Larry."

"You're easy to love, Lilly, and you know how to respond to them."

It was fun shopping with Ruth. We acted like two young "school girls" as we tried on dress after dress.

She decided on pale pink chiffon with a darker shade of pink flowers. It was very becoming and she reminded me of Teresa when she tried it on.

The brochure that Billy and Nathanael had put together was

attractive and informative. It was placed in offices and schools. As soon as it was distributed we began to receive inquiries.

The hours for the grand opening were 6 p.m. to 8 p.m. followed by a reception. That morning the family made a final inspection tour.

The wording engraved in the ironwork above the entrance gate was very impressive: "The Teresa Mathis Memorial Gardens and Eden Institute." The gardens were more beautiful than ever. Lee and his assistants had outdone themselves. The gardens could easily be ranked among the most beautiful and unique in the world, but of course, not the largest.

Lee's greenhouse was in the beginning stage, which would eventually contain rare specimens of flowers and plants to be propagated.

The foyer of the house led to the large living room highlighted by the grand piano in the center of the room. Around the room two small sofas and a number of chairs were placed in a manner to provide a home-like atmosphere and at the same time an aura of open space.

Beyond the living room was the dining room that had been left the same. It had sliding glass doors opening to a terrace overlooking the English garden. Later, we planned to serve afternoon tea by appointment on the terrace.

Teresa's bedroom had been transformed into the architecture and design classroom. David and Jeanine had hung pictures of Teresa's designs and buildings on the walls. A large worktable at one end of the room would be used for layouts and blue prints. An adjoining dressing room and closet had been converted to the classroom.

The room that Larry and Teresa had called the "special" guestroom was now the landscaping department. It had an outside entrance leading to the gardens.

Larry's bedroom became the conservation and environmental department, complete with screen and projector for showing documentaries and related films.

The library would consist of books pertaining to the three courses of study. It had already been partially stocked.

With very few changes the den became the conference room and

Larry's office was the business office for the institute.

I had spoken very little during the tour.

"What are you thinking, Lilly?" Larry said.

"It's perfect, absolutely perfect, and exactly as we planned."

"Yes, and it will be an asset to the community and a living, viable memory to Teresa."

Alexander, Josie, Peter and Naomi were in charge of the reception. Lee could hardly wait to start conducting the tour of the garden.

Several businesses and organizations had sent flower arrangements congratulating us. I was on cloud 9. The entire family was pleased but Sabrina was excited most of all.

"Lilly, I don't understand how so many changes have been made, but it still looks like Eden."

"Lots of planning, Sabrina, and hard work."

"I know what it is, Lilly—it's magic."

"I think you're right, Sabrina."

When I stop to reflect on my life, as I do so often, I've decided all of it has been magical. So...so much had happened in twenty-five years.

I've had it all—insecurity, frustration, sorrow, uncertainty, but lots of happiness. It takes all of these stirred together, mixed to the right consistency to make us who we need to be—compassionate, caring, loving, understanding and forgiving. Then it becomes as Sabrina says, "Magic."

For some reason I was very nervous trying to get dressed. I couldn't fasten the necklace.

"Larry, you'll have to put the necklace on me."

The dress was perfect with the earrings and necklace.

I had worried about wearing the necklace. I thought I might be sad, or maybe experience a bit of guilt, but that wasn't the case.

"Oh, Baby!" (Larry didn't call me baby very often. In fact, I could count the times on one hand, and always it had been during an emotional moment.) "Baby, I've never seen you look more beautiful."

I didn't want to cry and ruin my makeup, but it was no time to be concerned about makeup. If there was ever a time when Larry and I needed to be close and in each other's arms it was that moment.

There was a knock at the door. It was Sabrina.

"Granddaddy, Lilly, may I come in?"

She looked like an angel and Ruth was beaming. She looked lovely too.

"Let's go," Larry said, "we want to get there before our guests arrive."

Billy was talking with Joshua when we got there and Nathanael and Cecil were deep in conversation. I knew they were reminiscing about the past—taking a sentimental journey.

I enjoyed watching Billy and Joshua. My mind traveled back in time also when Billy and Joshua were young boys. They had always been close friends. Joshua realized he was a little different but he still had self esteem. He had been the mascot and errand boy of Sea Haven and he took his job seriously.

Now, he was living with and working for Cecil and his family. They had taken him in after his grandmother died.

"Miriam," I said, "it's great what you and Cecil have done for Joshua."

"He's an asset for us—a real blessing. Joseph adores him."

"Yes, it works both ways, doesn't it? Real fulfillment can be a matter of giving and receiving."

It was time to greet our guests. Billy, Jason, Ruth, Larry and I were the official hosts.

Jason played the piano during the reception and Amanda gave two violin solos. Nathanael had arranged for a harp to be brought in. Maria played beautifully. She had mastered the harp, which is very difficult.

Sabrina walked by. "Granddaddy," she said, "I think I'll get married here."

"Oh, really," teasing her he said, "have you picked out a husband?"

"Not yet, but I'm thinking about it. I may wait until Anthony grows up."

As she walked away, she turned around, apparently deep in thought, "Or I might wait for Joseph to grow up."

Larry and I smiled.

The weeks ahead were busy, and very hectic. We had already received inquiries about the various classes, more about landscaping than the other two.

The decision was made to start these classes first and later add the other two. We also opened the gardens to the public, by appointment, and Naomi and Josie served afternoon tea in the English Garden.

Jason and Ruth stayed two weeks longer, greeting the guests and explaining how much the garden had meant to their mother.

Sabrina asked if she could lead a group through the gardens representative of the Mediterranean.

"Please, please, I know the flowers of France and Italy."

"I don't think you know as much as you think you do. What will you do if they ask a question you can't answer?" Ruth asked her.

"I'll say I don't know and holler for Lee."

Larry spoke up, "What do you think, Lee?"

"You can do it, Sabrina, only if I can follow along with you. I won't interfere unless you ask me a question."

Sabrina was dancing all over the place. She turned out to be the most popular guide. One big problem—she didn't want to go home when Ruth said it was time.

There were still many legal matters to be worked out pertaining to private property being converted to public use. Special permission was needed so that Eden could be classified as an Institute of Higher Learning; an addendum provided that recitals and small concerts could be held there. The property was on a private road; therefore traffic was not a consideration.

Three and half months later classes started. The landscaping class had the limit of fifteen students, conservation had ten and architecture had six. The numbers would change from time to time.

The classes were arranged so that all three did not ever meet on the same day or at the same time.

For the first year Larry went to Eden a part of every day, but finally he said, "I want to spend more time at home with you, Lilly.

We're behind on sailing and sitting on our terrace."

"I know, I've thought the same thing. I've had an idea I want to run past you."

"What do you have in mind?"

"Let's sell 'Saunders Projections' and appoint Nathanael chief executive officer of Eden Institute. Lee and Peter would continue managing the gardens. What do you think?"

"I think it's a great idea if you're sure you want to do this."

"Yes, I'm sure. Nathanael has done an excellent job of managing 'Saunders Projections.'"

Nathanael was elated. The business was sold within two months. I thought to myself, how strange and interesting things had turned out.

Billy loved his work with "Protect the Earth Foundation"; he and his family were happy living at Canaan; life was good all the way around. Billy and Iris brought the children sailing often. Sometimes Larry and I sailed at the same time they did. It was a good way to bond with the grandchildren.

A year later Larry received a call from Ruth.

"Hi, Dad, how's everything?"

"Fine, honey, it's good to hear your voice. How's Sabrina?"

"Great! She wants to come to the States to live, that is, Santa Barbara."

"How do you feel about it?"

"I want to come, too. Life has been good in Naples but I miss my family. I need to be near you, Lilly, and the others."

"This is wonderful! What a surprise."

"Dad, is there a place for me at the Institute? I would like to be involved."

"Of course. What about your business there?"

"I have a good opportunity to sell for an unbelievable price. I would like to buy property near Eden."

"Unfortunately, Ruth, there isn't much turnover in that neighborhood, but I'll contact my real estate agent and see what we can come up with. It may take a while to find something but I'll call you when I have any information."

Two months later Leona, the real estate agent, called. I answered the phone.

"Lilly, I may have found a place your step-daughter would be interested in. Is Larry there?"

"No, he's at the Institute, but you can call him there."

"I'll tell you briefly about it and then you and Larry can discuss it. This property is located three or four miles from Eden, consisting of three and a half acres and a medium size house. The owners are an elderly couple who plan to move to a retirement home. It is going to be sold at auction in six weeks."

"It sounds like a possibility to me. Call Larry."

I didn't hear from Larry for over two hours. "I called Ruth after talking with Leona," he said. "She wants us to look at the property and call her."

Leona made arrangements with Mr. and Mrs. Parker, the owners. They had decided to sell at auction for two reasons—quick sale and not having to show the property day after day, which can be disturbing.

The rule of the auction was that prospective buyers could tour the property four days before the auction but they made an exception when Leona told them the situation.

The land and surrounding area was beautiful and the house was very nice, designed well, good flow of the rooms and the right size for Ruth and Sabrina. The only drawback—it was in need of repair.

The Parkers, because of age and physical disabilities, had not been able to keep it up.

Ruth liked our description of everything and said she would come for the auction.

A year later Ruth and Sabrina were in their new home. Larry appointed Ruth the Manager of the Institute, but she wore many hats.

Sabrina talked Lee into naming her, unofficially, of course, Assistant Tour Director of the Gardens.

The success of the Institute was phenomenal; the classes were at maximum capacity. Many clubs and organizations wanted to meet there. After discussions with Naomi and Josie we decided to serve lunch to small groups by appointment.

Afternoon tea would be served only on Tuesdays and Thursdays.

Now, Larry and I were free to enjoy our home more with the freedom to come and go to and from Eden.

Larry was asked to speak at conservation and environmental meetings held at the Institute. I sometimes spoke at garden club meetings assisted by Lee at times. Sabrina had learned topiary plant design from Lee. She wanted to give a demonstration at a garden club meeting and I was amazed at her ability, enthusiasm and poise.

Chapter 24

Now, sitting on the terrace looking out toward the channel, I see a schooner anchored at the pier resting between trips to the island. I see "The Water Baby" waiting for Larry and me; and I see my life passing in review like a panorama.

So many people have been a part of my life—some for only short periods of time while others are still an integral part of my life.

Jason and Maria visited us two or three times a year. Ruth and Sabrina were a joy to us.

Nathanael was the mainstay of the Institute and we considered him as family, just as we did Peter, Naomi and Lee.

Billy, our adopted son, had been a great blessing to us, giving us grandchildren. Alexander and Josie had made an indelible imprint on my life.

Numerous, interesting people had crossed my path in this magnificent journey of life and it wasn't over yet.

After all these years I still thrill at the sight of Larry, the love of my life. Our love is still glowing, the flame is not diminished. When we make love it is just as beautiful, wonderful and magical as the first time.

Finding the secret of love isn't always easy. Some people never find it in the true sense, perhaps because of unwillingness to make the sacrifice of complete selflessness and commitment.

It's never too late to uncover the secret. In fact, one must experience the deep valleys as well as the peaks before being seasoned and mature enough to know the true meaning and purpose of love.

Larry and I had traveled the same road but in different ways. We knew what it was to have unfulfilled desire. We had known the joy of life with another spouse and the sorrow when they were taken from us.

Now in our middle years we share simple pleasures, sailing with Sabrina, watching her expression as the breeze blows her hair, the excitement when Larry allows her to take the helm, playing games with the children as they learn the joy of simple things.

I hope Larry and I have many years yet to enjoy the sunrises and sunsets together, sharing unexpected joy in little things. For the time being I'm content to sleep in Larry's arms every night, and each morning watch the sails go up and the waves come ashore.